SEND NUDES

SEND NUDES

Stories

Saba Sams

BLOOMSBURY PUBLISHING

LONDON · OXFORD · NEW YORK · NEW DELHI · SYDNEY

BLOOMSBURY PUBLISHING
Bloomsbury Publishing Plc
50 Bedford Square, London, WC1B 3DP, UK
29 Earlsfort Terrace, Dublin 2, Ireland

BLOOMSBURY, BLOOMSBURY PUBLISHING and the Diana logo
are trademarks of Bloomsbury Publishing Plc

First published in Great Britain 2022

A catalogue record for this book is available from the British Library

ISBN: HB: 978-1-5266-2177-1; TPB: 978-1-5266-4898-3;
EBOOK: 978-1-5266-2178-8; EPDF: 978-1-5266-5222-5

2 4 6 8 10 9 7 5 3

Typeset by Integra Software Services Pvt. Ltd.
Printed and bound in Great Britain by CPI Group (UK) Ltd, Croydon CR0 4YY

To find out more about our authors and books visit www.bloomsbury.com
and sign up for our newsletters

For my grandmother Mimi
short for Miraculous

Yes, we were stupid for disrespecting the limits placed before us; for trying to go everywhere and know everything. Stupid, spoiled, and arrogant. But we were right, too. *I* was right.

Mary Gaitskill, Veronica

CONTENTS

Tinderloin

I met Ryan on Tinder. He only had one photograph of himself on his profile, edited with a grainy filter. I thought he looked alright. I didn't have much in the way of standards. My own picture wasn't even really me; it was another lanky brunette that I'd found online, her face turned away from the camera. My bio was *Tinderloin*, after my favourite cut.

We met in the Crown and Sceptre. I ordered wild boar sausages with mash and caramelised onion gravy. Ryan was older than me by eleven years. He worked for a cab service, picking up the phone. His hands were nice and thick, a good ratio of muscle to fat, and he'd crack his knuckles when there was a lull in conversation, or smooth out a napkin with his palms. When I told him about Papa's shop he joked that he was a vegetarian. I raised my eyebrows and smiled; I'd already overheard him order the roast chicken at the bar.

I went back to his after. He lived in his grandparents' garage. There was an electric heater groaning in the corner, and the corrugated iron door gave the place an industrial look. I felt at home in there; it reminded me of the shop in a way. A few carcasses wouldn't have looked so out of place, hung up next to his bookshelf.

When I slept with Ryan that first time I bled through the sheets. I was sixteen and I'd done my waiting.

A virgin then, are you? he'd said.

I'd just looked at him. There wasn't much point in lying. The blood had dried fast between my thighs and matted up my pubic hair, so the skin there pulled tight when I shuffled off the bed. The whole garage smelt of copper, like after opening a fresh pig.

I spent the next evening in the back of the shop with Papa, sawing a few lambs down into primals. We had Radio 4 on in the background. Papa likes *The Archers* so much he has the theme tune as his ringtone. If I speak during it he puts his blue-gloved hand up to silence me. I had to wait until the programme finished to tell him about Ryan.

I don't need to hear things like that, Gracie, he'd said.

He hadn't even let me finish.

It's not right, OK? Talking about those private moments with your old dad. Keep it to yourself in future.

It hadn't occurred to me that I shouldn't tell him, but then I was always doing things like that. I found it difficult to gauge certain situations. The day I got my first period I brought my knickers down to breakfast and laid them next to Papa's bowl of cornflakes, with the purple-brown smear facing him. I was beside myself. I thought I was dying.

Don't they teach you about all this in school, Gracie?

He'd picked up his cereal and was eating standing up, so to be further from my knickers. It came back to me then: all that stuff from PSHE about the menstrual cycle. I balled the knickers up in my pocket and went out to the back garden to set them on fire, in a sort of ceremony, and after that I went to school smelling like barbeque. I didn't have the money for tampons, so I just used screwed-up wads of tissue paper for that whole first year, until Papa started paying me to do Saturdays in the shop.

My mother died when I was six. I have a memory of being in the supermarket and losing her. I threaded up and down every aisle to look, and then I found her by the freezers. I was so relieved I could feel my heart throbbing in the roof of my mouth. She had her back to me.

She was wearing a purple walking jacket and had her hand in with the ice creams. I ran up and put my arms around her thighs, pressed my face against her.

Honey, she said. I'm not sure you've got the right person.

I looked up at her and she wasn't my mother at all. She was much older in the face, and she had a few burst blood vessels under her eyes, like tiny jellyfish. I jumped. I wanted to scream but the noise wouldn't come up in my throat, so I just turned and ran as fast as I could down the aisle. I bumped into a man with a pot of yoghurt, and I knocked it from his hand. It split and went all over the floor, but I didn't stop running.

I can't remember how I found my mother again, but I suppose I must have. She didn't die until the year after that.

The sex hadn't gone how I'd imagined, but it had *gone*, and that was the main thing. I walked around that week feeling slightly lighter on my feet. I passed a mock GCSE paper in my maths class, which hadn't happened before. I performed very well at my butchery. Papa couldn't believe the consistency of my sirloins. He said he'd never seen anything like it, and even I have to admit they were quite lovely.

The weekend after we first met, Ryan and I went on a country walk around a stately home that had its grounds open to the public. He drove me there with his dog, Petal, in the back. I'd brought Ryan a few nice chops wrapped in greaseproof, as a gift, and I was devastated when he fed one to Petal. She was one of those chunky breeds with skin so tight that you could see the shape of her skull under it. I watched the muscles of her jaw working away at the chop and thought of all the effort I'd put into separating them, the careful layer of fat I'd left, thick as orange peel.

On the walk, Petal either tried to start fights with other dogs or barked at sheep through the wire fence. She had a taste for them now, that much was clear. When we got back to the car park, Ryan and I had sex on the back seats. Petal sat in front of the steering wheel and watched us through the headrests.

There's a good girl, Ryan kept saying. I wished he was talking to me.

It was a month later that I found out I was pregnant. I was in the shop, and the smell coming up off the mincer was so intense I had to run out to the street to throw up into the gutter.

Take a test, said Papa, when I returned.

I wiped my mouth on the sleeve of my workwear. It took me a moment to understand what he was saying, and when I did I turned and walked back outside again. My vomit was a thin, yellow bile on the tarmac.

The man behind the counter in the pharmacy looked embarrassed when I asked to use the toilet, but I'd already paid for the test so he let me. The two red lines flashed up immediately, clear as smit marks. I must have fallen asleep then, because the next thing I knew I was curled on the floor of the cubicle, my forehead pressed against the cold porcelain of the toilet, and the man was knocking on the door to check on me. I have no idea how long I was lying there.

I told Papa straight away. He was shaping some of the mince into burgers and he didn't look up. The meat squelched in his hands as he spoke.

It'll happen, that, he said. We'll get you sorted.

We made the call that evening. The receptionist at the clinic booked me an appointment for two weeks' time. They didn't have anything available sooner. Papa sat at the kitchen table with me during the conversation, and when I hung up we shared one of his pork pies with lots of mustard. They've won awards, those pies. Papa had special stickers made. I've asked, but he won't give me the recipe. He says that when he dies, those pies will die with him.

I didn't make it to the abortion. I'm not sure I would have anyway; I'd been having second thoughts. I'd started to switch off in lessons, or mid-conversation with Papa. I'd find myself imagining a little baby, fast asleep in my arms. When I eventually came around, I'd realise I had no idea what had been happening in the real world. I once found myself in a corner shop, buying chewing gum, with no memory of how I'd got there. Still, the decision was made for me, in the end. When the blood first started it was a very bright, garish red. I was in school, in the lunch queue, when a boy called Oliver pointed at me.

Someone's got the painters in, he shouted.

I went home and stayed there. The blood got heavier and heavier over days, and the rest came out in pieces, alongside some of the worst cramps I've ever experienced. Some of the pieces were stringy and some more circular, dark and shiny as kidneys. I knew enough about flesh to know it was the baby.

It didn't stop until Saturday. That morning, in the shop, Papa said I looked pale. He sent me into the back to get on with some French trimming. I was using a boning knife that I'd sharpened the day before. The blade gleamed in the sunlight coming in through the little window. For the first time in weeks, the rack of lamb smelt bearable. I took the tip of the blade and pressed it into my left thumb on the chopping board. It broke the nail easily. I felt the knife scrape the top of the bone before breaking through to the other side. I pulled it out again. There was a horizontal cut almost the width of the nail, and just a pinprick at the back, where the tip of the blade had made it through. Blood spilt all over the chopping board and the floor. I could actually see it pumping; there was a definite rhythm to it. I used some blue roll to bandage my thumb. The pain was steady and vivid. I felt OK then, I felt almost normal.

I'd been seeing Ryan regularly. We'd spend time in his garage, watching films and having sex. He had a camping stove attached to a gas canister in the corner, and in the mornings, before school, he'd fry eggs with some back bacon I'd brought from Papa's shop. Ryan didn't have a toaster, so he'd put the bread in the pan too and let it crisp up in the fat. Petal would get a portion about the size of mine, and Ryan would get double.

I'd decided not to tell him about the pregnancy, but the first time I visited after I miscarried I could tell that Petal knew. She climbed up on the bed and put her head in my lap. I scratched her behind the ears with my good hand and she smiled with her tongue spilling out her mouth. This was the first time we'd ever really acknowledged each other, and Ryan was impressed.

I've not seen her like that with anyone other than me, he said.

Ryan made us White Russians with some milk he kept in a mini fridge. I'd never had a cocktail before, and I felt grown up with it. I drank very carefully, trying to move as little of my body as possible so as not to wake

Petal, who had fallen asleep on me. I sat like that for hours, and when I complained of backache Ryan gave me a massage. His big fingers digging into me weren't necessarily soothing, but I'd never felt closer to him. Petal's snores wheezed through the silence. She was warm as a running engine.

The next day, we went for a walk on the hill that overlooked the town. I threw sticks for Petal with my good hand. She chased them down and returned them foamy with saliva. Ryan carried on ahead with his hands pressed into his pockets. Eventually Petal bored of me and dropped her sticks at his feet instead. Ryan could throw much further than I could. After, he looked back at me and winked.

She's playing the field, he said.

I laughed, then spent the rest of the walk trying to catch Petal's eye. I wanted her to bring the sticks to me again, but she didn't.

We went to a pub after. I ordered a bowl of water for Petal and a pint for myself. The barman asked for my ID, but Ryan just put his hand on my shoulder.

Alright mate, he said. She's with me.

We sat in the garden with our drinks. Ryan ripped open a bag of pork scratchings and lay the packet out on the picnic table. He'd drop one to Petal every so often, and she'd catch it in her jaws and crunch it to dust. It was late afternoon by then and cold, so I took my jacket off and covered Petal with it. Goose pimples surfaced quickly on my arms, and when Ryan noticed he slipped his own coat off and passed it to me. It was so huge it drowned me, and for the first time in my life I felt cute. We sat like that, in our swapped clothes, way into the evening.

I didn't get home until past dark. Papa was waiting up in the living room.

Grace, he said. Jesus. I've been pulling my hair out.

I told him I was sorry. I hadn't thought about him all day and I felt terrible.

You were with him again, weren't you? he said.

Yes, Papa.

Papa smoothed out his frown with the tops of his fingers. You just look out for yourself, won't you Gracie?

Yes, Papa, I said, and then I went to bed.

After injuring my thumb, I lost touch with my butchery for a while. I'd had the wound patched up properly at the hospital, but for weeks after I was still slow with my knife work, and this made me frustrated and inaccurate. At school, I couldn't write, so I just sat in the back of my lessons and looked off out the window. The teachers didn't notice; I'd mostly always done that anyway.

Papa seemed a little hurt every time I presented him with my cuts, but he'd put them in the counter without saying anything. I busied myself in the shop by packing treats for Petal instead. I'd never been much of a dog person, but she'd charmed me that weekend. I'd bag up some offal while Papa wasn't looking, or cut a few sausages from their string. I once brought her an entire beef hind shank. I'd stayed behind to close up shop, and before I left I stole it out the back, then walked over to Ryan's with it balanced on my shoulder like a Flintstone.

I was spending most nights with them by that point, and when I arrived Petal would run out of the garage to greet me. I'd lay her gifts down on the front lawn and watch her devour them, and then we'd go in together to see Ryan, Petal leaving a trail of pink saliva behind us.

It didn't take long for Petal to become protective of me. I understood that she'd learnt to associate me with good fresh meat, but I like to think that our bond ran deeper than her stomach. We felt comfortable around each other, was what it was.

She'd growl whenever Ryan touched me. It got to the point where it was easier just to wait until she was distracted outside or asleep on her mat. I didn't mind this; there was something romantic about it to me.

She loves you so much, Ryan whispered once. He was leaning over my body to check that the coast was clear.

I invited Ryan and Petal over to meet Papa one evening. It was six weeks or so after the miscarriage, and my thumb was fully healed. I baked the same chicken and mushroom pies that we sell in the shop. Evening light through the lace curtains dappled the whole dining room. Ryan put his glass down without a coaster, and Papa waited until he was in the toilet to slip one underneath. Petal sat up at the dining table with us and licked her plate clean. I felt proud of her.

See Papa, I said. Isn't she well behaved?

Papa nodded. She's a lovely dog.

Ryan and I reached out at exactly the same time and stroked either side of Petal's face. She was sitting between us. She turned her head to me first, and then to Ryan. There was a bead of gravy in her whisker, and she used her tongue to get it. We all laughed.

She loves being the centre of attention, I said.

I can see that, said Papa.

After, we played Gin Rummy in the living room. Papa took two games and I took one. Ryan was slow with his cards and kept getting the spade confused with the club. Petal lay on the floor. A fire was going, and she looked pleased with the heat on her belly.

When they were leaving, Papa shook Ryan's hand and then went to pat Petal. She barked once and sunk her teeth into his ankle.

I'm so sorry, said Ryan. She's not good with new people.

I got down on eye level with Petal and told her to behave herself. She looked ashamed, so I gave her a quick rub under the chin. Papa wasn't one to make a fuss, but from down there I could see a few dark spots of blood coming up through his trousers.

Ryan's cousin was getting married in Wales the following weekend, and he'd asked me to have Petal while he was away. I waited until the Thursday to tell Papa this. He was still walking with a limp, and I had to bring a chair out front in the shop so that he could sit down to rest when there weren't any customers. He wasn't enthusiastic about having Petal to stay, but I told him it was too late for Ryan to find someone else.

I'd started getting excited about work again, now that my thumb was better. I'd go straight from school to the shop. I had half a pig to practise my seam butchery on, and the roasts came out beautiful. Papa cheered up when I showed him, but it didn't last long. One afternoon, he caught me sneaking a whole rack of spare ribs for Petal.

Can't you just give her the trotters? he said, clicking his tongue.

She needs some comfort this weekend, Papa. It's unsettling, staying in a new place.

Papa shook his head. Half of those ribs back, at least.

I was stroppy, but I divided the rack into two and put one on show in the cabinet.

That weekend with Petal was wonderful. I fried up a whole tube of black pudding and we shared it. We spent Saturday afternoon walking. I took her to a field of long grasses and watched her weave through them like a snake, leaving a stepped-down trail behind her. The sun was so bright it made the dew dazzling. After, tired out, Petal leant against me with all her weight and panted. Her thick tail slapped at my thighs. I picked a tick off her back, squashed it between my knuckles, and her warm blood ran down my thumb like ink from a cartridge.

We shared a bed that night. If I rolled too close her sour breath would wake me, but when Sunday morning streamed in the first thing I saw was Petal. She smiled at me and squinted. I stroked her belly and rubbed my face into her neck.

On Sundays, I always went and helped Papa prep the carcasses for the rest of the week. I'd been doing this since I was very small, it's how I learnt all my knife skills. I brought Petal that weekend. She sat quietly under the counter, twitching her ears occasionally when something good happened on *The Archers*, leaving shiny patches behind on the linoleum when she licked up the scraps I dropped for her.

She's got a real appetite, that dog.

Hasn't she, Papa?

It's nice to see you so close to someone, Gracie, I must say.

Yes, Papa.

Ryan, I mean.

Oh. Yes, Papa.

How old is he, Grace?

Twenty-seven, Papa.

Papa got a ball of string out from a drawer and started to cut it into equal lengths. I used them to tie a few roasts. Neither of us spoke much for the rest of the afternoon.

Petal was confused when Ryan came back that evening. I think she was under the impression that I'd be looking after her full-time from now on. She whined when he clipped the lead to her collar, and I felt so guilty I could barely look. We were in my house, just by the front door.

Why don't I come stay with you tonight? I said to Ryan. You know, settle her in.

Ryan had just driven all the way from Wales, and he was impatient to get home. He looked irritated, but he agreed to have me. I got in the back of the car with Petal to reassure her. She kept looking up at me while we were driving, to check I was still there.

When we got to the garage, Petal curled up in her bed and Ryan opened Netflix on his laptop. He liked having something on all the time, even just as background noise. We talked briefly about the wedding, and I told him in lots of detail what Petal and I had been up to.

You spoil her, he said.

I smiled. It was true.

We waited for Petal's snores before we started. I was used to having sex most days by then, and my appetite for it had exploded. I rubbed Ryan through his jeans, and chewed on his earlobe. He let me get on with this, but his hands stayed limp on the mattress.

Touch me, I said.

I'm so tired, Grace.

I looked at him. His eyes were slightly purple underneath. I'd never been to a wedding, but I understood that they could take a lot out of you. Still, I was overexcited. I lay down on the mattress and pulled him onto me.

Ryan, I said. Let's.

He seemed reluctant, but he did lean in to kiss me. The weight of his body on mine made me feel crushed and helpless. I closed my eyes and moaned. This was always when I liked Ryan best: just before the sex. Most other times I didn't find the things that he did particularly interesting. I helped him get his jeans off and then my own. I could feel him through his boxers. He smelt of Parma ham and polythene. My whole body was throbbing. I cried out for him.

In hindsight, I was probably being louder than I should have. Petal was on the bed so fast. Before I could even register what was happening, Ryan let out a sharp yelp that ripped through the garage. She'd gone straight for his forearm. Her jaw was scissored around it. He tried to pull away, but Petal's grip was locked. He gasped and twisted. Thick, red droplets collected on the bed sheets, and I could see bits of Ryan's arm flapping, soft and pink as raw chicken.

Petal, I shouted. Petal.

She dropped him then, finally. She came down off the bed and stood at my feet. A string of Ryan's skin was dangling from her jaw, dripping. I was struggling to breathe at a normal pace. Ryan was making weak, insignificant grunts on the bed. His face was expressionless, a very pale grey, and he was holding his arm as if it were a baby. There was as much blood as I've ever seen, and I've seen blood. It seeped into the mattress, slow as oil. I just stood and watched. Time felt still. Petal lifted her head to me. She blinked, licked her lips and grinned, her eyes half-closed with pleasure. She looked euphoric in that moment.

Ryan's grandparents burst in soon after that. They must have heard my screams. I was naked still, backed into the corner, trying to cover my body with my hands. Ryan's grandfather tossed me a T-shirt from the floor, and didn't look in my direction again.

I'm Grace, I said.

No one responded. Ryan's grandmother was pacing the room, shaking her hands. Ryan's grandfather pulled a pillowcase off a pillow and used it to wrap up Ryan's arm. The blood was so red against the white it looked fake.

Fucking dog, he muttered. That thing needs putting down.

I burst into tears then. Once I was crying, I couldn't stop. Ryan's grandparents took us both outside and put us in the car. The night was purple. Petal stayed behind. I could hear her whining as we drove down the street. Ryan's grandfather dropped Ryan off at the hospital with his grandmother, and then he took me home. I didn't speak the whole way, I just wept and wept.

When I got inside, Papa came straight out of his bedroom. He was in his tartan pyjamas, and he looked barely awake.

Gracie, he said. My god. What's happened?

I looked down at myself. I was still wearing only Ryan's T-shirt, and there were specks of blood on my bare legs and feet. My face, I knew, would be puffed up from crying.

Nothing, Papa. I'm fine.

Papa's mouth did something then that I'd never seen before. It quivered, and I thought he might suddenly become very angry, or very sad. It only lasted a second, and then he was holding me in his arms, stroking my hair with one of his palms. The hug was so tight I almost couldn't breathe, and then he let me go.

You're not seeing that Ryan again, Grace. I don't like it. I won't have it.

But Papa—

No.

I turned away from him and went into my bedroom. He stood and watched me go. I didn't see any point in arguing. It wasn't Ryan I needed anyway; it was Petal.

School the next day felt longer than ever. I called Ryan between every lesson, and then again at lunch, sitting in front of a blue tray while my gravy coagulated. Each time, he didn't pick up. I skipped my last lesson of the afternoon and went to see him. I'd never disobeyed Papa before, and the feeling of it made me nauseous. I knocked straight on the corrugated iron door of the garage, and Ryan took a long time to come and fold it open.

Hi, I said.

His arm was wrapped in white bandages, held at a right angle in a gauze sling. I don't think he'd slept since I'd seen him last.

You look awful, I said.

Thanks.

I leant forward and gave him a kiss on the corner of his mouth. When my lips touched him, he flinched. I knew he didn't want my company, but I went into the garage anyway. The sheets had been changed, and there were some packets of pain medication on the chair. My clothes from the day before had been neatly folded in the exact spot on the floor where I'd left them. The dog bed was empty.

Where's Petal?

Ryan shook his head. He seemed angry at the question. She attacked me, Grace.

I know that.

She's not safe.

She was confused.

Listen, said Ryan. We're sending her away.

I fell apart then. I stopped being able to see clearly; my vision filled with grey dots. I started to pick things up from around the room and throw them. I ripped all the hangers from the clothes rail. I emptied a pen pot onto the concrete floor. I unplugged a whole row of electrical items and hurled them at the opposite wall. Ryan didn't intervene.

Where is she? I screamed.

Please, Ryan said. He kept saying it, quietly, over and over.

I stopped destroying the room and collapsed onto the bed. I felt drained of energy. My face was covered in tears and snot. I kicked my school shoes up and down against the mattress. My sobs became weak and breathy. The garage was completely silent, other than that. Ryan hadn't moved from his position by the door. It was then, just as I was starting to calm down, that I heard the bark.

Petal, I shouted. Petal!

The barks kept coming. She could hear me. I started to cry again. I could almost feel her tongue, rough and wet on my hands.

Take me to her, I said.

Ryan folded his arms. I knew that I would never see him again, after this, and I didn't care. Just let me see her, I said.

Ryan turned and walked out of the garage. I followed him across the front lawn to his grandparents' front door. I'd never been inside the house before. The hall was full of old-people furniture. There were paintings of fruit bowls hung up on the walls. If his grandparents were in, I didn't see them. I could hear Petal whimpering, and I ran to her. She was in the living room, in a cage pushed into the corner. I knelt at her level and stuck my hands through the bars to touch her. She looked uncomfortable in there, hunched over herself. I wished I'd brought a treat.

Petal, I said. Petal, my love.

She had sleep crusted into the corners of her eyes, as if she'd been weeping. She looked up at me and whined. I couldn't stop myself. I flicked open the lock on the cage, and Petal flew out. She leapt into me and pushed me backwards onto the musty carpet. I lay under her, my arms wrapped around her solid middle. We stayed like that for ages. I just held her.

When Petal let me get up, I noticed Ryan had left the room. He must have been worried that she'd bite him again. I went and opened the door to the living room, to find him standing in the hall. He looked so scared, I was embarrassed for him. Petal sat obediently at my feet.

Let me take her, I said.

No. She's dangerous.

I rolled my eyes.

Your dad wouldn't have it, said Ryan. She could kill him, Grace.

I shrugged. Deep down, I knew that that was true. I looked at Ryan properly for the first time. He seemed to soften in front of me.

Please, I tried.

Grace. I'm not going to let them put her down, alright? But she needs expert care.

Petal moaned a little, as if she understood. I felt cruel, for talking about her as if she wasn't in the room.

I don't believe you, I said to Ryan.

I stepped around him, and started towards the front door. It was made of heavy wood, and I had to use both hands to get it open. As soon as I did, the late afternoon sunlight flooded in. It picked up all the dust. Ryan was stood deep into the hall, next to a coat stand, and Petal was between the two of us, turning her head back and forth. Whenever she faced me, her eyes caught the sunlight. They looked completely clear, amber as two fallen leaves.

Where will you take her? Ryan said.

I didn't answer. It didn't matter. We could do anything, Petal and I. We could go to Scotland and walk the hills. We could go to Rome and eat spaghetti. We could go to Barcelona and bathe in the frothy sea. I'd send postcards to Papa all about it, but Petal and I wouldn't be back.

See you, I said to Ryan, and then I walked away. After a few steps, I looked back over my shoulder and whistled.

Overnight

Maxine saw him first through the viewfinder of her Snapchat. His face was far-off, turned in the opposite direction to the rest of the crowd, so the strobes picked him out like a full moon. She zoomed in, pulled him into focus, watched for a while. His hair was longer. He'd shaved three slits into his left eyebrow. He was turned to talk to a girl, tall, dancing slightly behind him. They were sharing a Red Stripe.

Maxine put her phone in her bra and shouldered her way outside. The sky was all frothy blues and pinks. Sunrise had come around fast. She found a corner of the smoking area to roll a cigarette, her ears ringing out into the cold.

His name was George. Maxine had met him in Primark, the final day of summer before the first day of secondary school. Their mums had got chatting while shopping for uniforms, last minute and on the cheap.

You know the school shop? Charges sixteen pound a polo.

The cheeky bastard fuckers.

So they'd stood side by side in silence, their eyes on the floor, as trousers were held to their narrow hips, shirt sleeves pulled tight along the lengths of their arms. Maxine could hear George's iPod shuffle, very faint, left going in his jacket.

Jesus wept. Look at the queue for the changing rooms.

Size up Georgie, we're not doing this next year.

Afterwards, outside, while their mums smoked ciga-rettes and laughed like they'd known each other for years, George had pressed one of his earphones into Maxine's palm, and together they'd listened to Sean Kingston's 'Beautiful Girls', peering out from under their hoods as the late afternoon light made stripes on the pavement.

Alright love, let's get this bus.

You'll look out for each other you two, won't you?

Maxine had only been at the club a few hours. They'd stumbled across it on their way back from a house party shut down by noise complaints. Jos, the friend Maxine had come with, had disappeared a while back. Maxine had assumed that Jos had sloped off home, but she noticed her now through the haze of the smoking area, crouched low and crawling across the black concrete.

Jos.

Max, hey.

You OK down there?

Yep, all good, just lost an earring.

Oh right, when?

Fucking ages, no idea.

Bit shit.

Yeah.

Maxine helped Jos to her feet, waited as she rubbed her palms up and down on her jeans. The dirt was thick as tar, almost glossy in the new daylight.

You got any wipes or anything?

There's sinks inside.

You know what Max, I'll just have one more look. They'll be here somewhere.

Sure.

Maxine dropped her cigarette to the ground and stepped on it. There was nothing for her to do now but go back inside. On the dance floor, George had turned to face the DJ. His head bobbed gently to the music. Maxine leant against the far wall at the opposite end of the room, next to the door. The crowd had cleared a little while she'd been smoking, so that if George were to turn around he'd see her. She stood with her body reeled in like a kite, waiting.

Maxine was thirteen when her dad moved out. It was then that she'd ended up spending a lot more time with George. Although in school George and Maxine rarely even passed nods in the corridors, their mums had stayed in touch, and long Saturdays spent knocking around each other's bedrooms had made George's flat a familiar second base. The lift up to his floor smelt of piss and he was three bus stops further down the route, but anywhere was better than home in those days, when Maxine's mum shredded up the evenings with her shouting and crying.

Stop calling him now, please stop.

Why?

He won't pick up, you know he won't.

It's not that. It's the answer machine. I like to listen to his voice.

Mum.

Let me hear his voice.

At George's, Maxine would sit collecting the grime condensed in the grooves of the kitchen table with her fingernail, while George played on his Nintendo DS. At around six, his mum would come home in her leopard coat with polystyrene kebab boxes, and the three of them would sit at the table, eating meat in ribbons and laughing. George didn't have a dad either. After they'd eaten, his mum would pull the cushions off the sofa and make a bed on the floor for Maxine, where she'd sleep in her uniform, a hot water bottle pulled up beneath her sweatshirt. In the middle of the night, she was often woken by George climbing in beside her.

Can't sleep again.

How come?

Don't know. But it helps sometimes, the sound of your breathing.

Jos followed Maxine inside after five minutes or so and began working her way around the edges of the room, using the torch on her phone to light up the floor. Maxine didn't move from her place against the wall, where she watched Jos scurry around like an oversized rat, the back of George's head nodding incessantly in the background, slightly faster now to keep in time with the beat.

Maxine thought back to the last place she'd seen George. Two Christmases ago, out of the window of her mum's car. He was walking out a Sainsbury's, something long and white in his mouth that Maxine took for a cigarette, then realised was a lollipop.

Was that George back there Max?

No, no, don't think so.

You sure? Looked just like him.

Positive.

The DJ let the last song run out to nothing. The over-head lights were turned on abruptly, so the whole room lit up filthy and stale. Maxine watched as everyone began to file out of the club, except Jos, who hadn't seemed to notice. Some people went to the bar for more drinks but were turned away. The girl that George was with spent a long time untying her jacket from around her waist and pulling it on. George stood waiting, holding her bag out for her to take when she was ready. They were among the last people left on the dance floor. Maxine took a step forward, out of the shadow cast by the far wall. George turned finally to face her. He looked up. His eyes settled on Maxine for a moment, then flicked across to the door on her right. Maxine would have questioned if he'd seen her, but she could tell by the way his ears stung red. She let her head swivel, almost of its own accord, so that her eyes could follow him all the way out of the room. He watched the door, unblinking, until he was through it. At one point, he passed so close that she could see the fine, soft hairs on the back of his neck.

Afterwards, when she was sure he had gone, she sunk down into the floor and sat with her eyes closed, her chin resting on her knees.

It was the summer between year nine and ten, when all the boys smelt of Lynx Africa and Subway. Maxine was a few months from turning fifteen. Her mum had a new boyfriend and a set of boy-girl twins. She seemed very happy and very tired, a book folded back against its spine. Maxine spent most days at home helping. She'd slice cucumbers into sticks that the babies carried off in their mouths to stash behind the couch, where later she'd fish the pieces out again, sogged and linty.

This was also the summer of drinking. George, whose mum stayed out late at weekends, would host small gatherings when the park was rained off. Maxine didn't show at most, but to one she did.

This one. Everyone sitting in a circle with the rain pounding out against the windows. The drink mostly cheap vodka mixed with rip-off Fanta, or that blue WKD. Someone with wine stolen from their parents, finally got open by pushing the cork down into the bottle with the blunt end of a lighter. A box of straights, found in a drawer in the kitchen and shared about the room. Two people sick by eleven, one in the toilet and the other in the shower. Maxine and George sharing an armchair, his hand moving up and down her thigh.

You never come around anymore.

Stop touching me like that.

Have another drink.

Is there vodka still?

There is.

And then the next morning, suddenly. Maxine woke with a taste in her mouth like an ashtray, George's shapes under the sheets, the sound of a fly dying against the window, a thick bruise across her left hip, and blood, on the tissue after the toilet.

What have you done?

What do you mean?

His face blank but for a light smirk, his head shaking slowly, his palms turned upwards in front of him. So she left, walked home through the park, with an image in her head that wouldn't shift: her body as a nut cracked open.

Come on girls, we're closing up shop.

Maxine raised her head to find the club almost completely deserted. She was alone other than Jos, searching through a pile of beer cans in the corner, and the bouncer who was kicking them out.

Been a big night, has it?

No, I'm fine.

Maxine lifted herself to standing and walked slowly outside, through the smoking area, onto the street and down to the bus stop. Commuters sat lined up neat in their cars. Birds tweeted. Jos caught up, swung her arm around Maxine's shoulders.

Sorry I wasn't around much tonight.

That's OK.

They weren't even pricey.

Some things are hard to let go of.

Yeah.

On the bus, they sat top deck at the very front so that it felt like they were driving. The sky bloomed huge and blue above them. Maxine picked at the crust of mascara hanging onto her eyelashes and looked out across the park, where thousands of new daisies had sprung up without warning, overnight.

Snakebite

Lara liked a snakebite. She drank other things but this was her go-to. She was only in it to get fucked; she didn't care about the taste. She admitted that to me freely, once I got to know her. I took a light interest in taste myself, but mostly I chose my booze by colour. I liked anything vibrant: Aperol or crème de menthe. I worked in a pub called the Queen's Head, and whenever things got depressing in there I'd pour myself a shot. My manager, Mark, rarely noticed. Unless the schoolgirls were in, he spent most of his time in the back, gambling on his own fruit machines.

I'd had six shots the night I met Lara. It was Valentine's Day. The pub was empty but for a single regular sat at the bar, reviewing his reflection in a pint of Guinness. The door opened and a guy came in, Lara following behind. It was raining out. They were both dripping gently, holding themselves. He was perhaps nineteen, in an ugly red and yellow polo shirt, no coat. He had an Adam's apple like a swallowed blade, hair in a scraggly ponytail. Lara wore fishnets and huge black boots. She seemed to be surrounded by a fine blue light.

It was only when the guy with the ponytail repeated his order that I realised I hadn't been listening. There was an edge of shyness to his voice, left over from being with Lara. The raindrops coming off him tapped at the wood floor.

Sorry, I said, reaching for the pint glasses.

It's lager and cider. Equal parts. Cheapest you've got.

I know what a snakebite is, I said.

He watched me, dead behind the eyes, as I poured. I was wearing a university hoodie, a rain mac, leggings worn thin at the crotch. My hair was clotted with grease, and there was nothing on my face but lip balm. I'd never had a boyfriend, and had just accepted it as the sort of thing that wouldn't happen to me. I imagined myself married, ten years down the line, to a man who used gel in his hair and cooked burgers on a barbeque for our dumpy kids, but I hadn't put much thought into how I might get there. The future, to me, was something that would just happen.

The guy with the ponytail paid in change, then went over to the pool table. He rested his drinks on the felt while he pushed coins into the slot. Lara went to him, lifted a snakebite and drank from it. She looked directly at me, just for a second, over the lip of her glass. Then she put the drink down and polished her cue with a chalk. She broke, and she broke well. The sound echoed through the room like a smashed glass.

The Queen's Head was a grotty pub, with streaky glasses and an odd assortment of furniture that had mostly been dragged in off the street. Mark notoriously didn't ask teenage girls for their IDs so they'd come from all over the city to get served, some not even bothering to change out of their uniforms first. Pervy Mark, they'd whisper to each other, while he used his teeth to crack open their Smirnoff Ices.

I'd dropped an empty CV into the Queen's Head midway through my first year, and got the job on the spot. I hadn't needed the money as much as something to do. University, it turned out, was little more than an empty time slot in which young people could take a stab at small-scale alcoholism before deciding whether or not to launch into the real thing. Halls, where I'd lived in my first year, radiated the slightly sweet smell of vomit. Patches of it would go unclaimed in the corridor for days, until eventually someone had the sense to run a hoover over them.

In my opinion, drinking was fine, but it wasn't an activity in and of itself. It didn't count as *doing something*. I'd come to university to meet the sort of people who wore berets, stole handfuls of cherries from fruit stalls, talked about art and politics. Here, rugby boys downed entire bottles of rosé followed by bowls of their own piss, then did press-ups in circles.

For my second year, I'd moved in with a group of medics, all female, with various skin conditions that they would discuss at length. They'd spend evenings on the sofa together watching *Take Me Out*, splitting a Domino's and scratching each other's arms.

E45? they'd say. Sudocrem? Bio-Oil?

When I went home to my parents' house in the Cotswolds for term holidays, a guy called Quaver would take over my shifts. He was at university elsewhere, but his parents lived opposite the Queen's Head, so he'd return to the city just as I was leaving. We'd crossed paths a few times. In early January, I showed up to my first shift of the year to find him standing on a chair, pulling down the tinsel that I'd stapled up a month before. He had a lip piercing and his hair was shaved and bleached yellow. He called me Babe, lazily, as he was leaving, then helped himself to a packet of peanuts from behind the bar. I remember thinking that Quaver could have been me, in a parallel universe.

When the game of pool was over, they sat at the corner table again. Lara had her back to me, so all I could see was the triangle of her elbow on the arm of the chair. The guy with the ponytail bought all the drinks. They moved on to lagers after the snakebites, and kept going for hours.

In this time, I drank two vodka cranberries and inhaled a supermarket pasta salad that I'd brought in my bag. I hand-washed all the pint glasses, sprayed the entire bar with Dettol and wiped it down. I took all the spirits off the shelves, dusted them and put them back. I checked my phone about once a minute, just for something to do. I went to the toilet a lot. My whole body was jittery and feverish. If I wasn't stealing glances at Lara, I was thinking about when I'd next get away with it.

At around eleven o'clock, Mark came over for a Strongbow. She's too fit for him, I reckon, he whispered into my ear.

I picked up a cloth and set to work polishing the taps, which I'd already done twice in the past hour. I hadn't noticed, I stuttered.

At last orders, I went over to Lara's table, my fingernails dug into my palms. Lara looked up and smiled. She seemed very drunk by then – her eyes were drooping – but that smile was perfect, glinting like a coin in the dim pub light.

You're on my course, she said.

I, um.

Anthropology?

Yes.

Thought I'd seen you around.

My fingertips felt slightly wet. Sorry, I said. I don't recognise—

It's cool, my attendance is shit. I'm almost never in.

Right, I said. Same.

This wasn't true. I always went to my lectures. I was actually quite fearful of what might happen if I didn't. It wasn't that I was worried about getting into trouble, more that I'd be completely forgotten, that I'd disappear.

You're cute.

It came out of nowhere, like a trick. I thought it was, at first.

Isn't she cute?

The guy with the ponytail looked me up and down.

So, er, it's last orders, I said.

What's your name? asked Lara.

For a moment, I forgot even this simple thing. Meg, I said finally. Yours?

She told me, and I started to turn away. I wanted to get back behind the bar, to safety.

Wait, Lara called. We should hang out.

I turned back. I was struggling to concentrate.

I need a girl mate, she explained. Too many boys around, you know?

I nodded as if that resonated with me.

Here, she said. Put your number in. We can get pissed.

Lara had one of those brick phones that could be dropped from any height and survive. It was battered at the edges. I punched in digits. My fingers were numb, perhaps someone else's.

I'll text you, she said.

I went back to the bar and started getting everything together for close. I did two shots of blue curaçao, just to calm down. I got the mop out and started sloshing it around the sticky floor behind the bar.

Later, Meg.

I said bye, but I didn't look up until I guessed Lara was almost out the door. Her ankles were unsteady, crossing over each other in their huge black boots. Once I got to know Lara, I noticed she wore those boots all the time. The girls I'd met before would put high heels on to go clubbing, and walk home barefoot with mascara running down their faces. Lara wouldn't have worn heels to a wedding, and I certainly never saw her cry.

The guy with the ponytail was propping her up with his arm. He touched her like she belonged to him. She wouldn't text me, I thought, as I watched her silhouette waver in the glass panels of the door.

◆

I received a text that Saturday. It was three o'clock in the afternoon and I was in bed fully clothed, eating

own-brand cheese puffs with stained fingers. Lara wanted
to meet at a karaoke bar, eight o'clock that evening.

The venue had red walls, a fuzzy projector displaying
YouTube lyrics onto one. Lara sang 'Angels' by Robbie
Williams, but she made it punky, somehow. She was
wearing red lipstick one shade darker than the walls. The
crowd loved it. She had us in the palm of her hand. At my
turn, I refused to sing. I told her I didn't know any lyrics.

That's the point of the screen, she said. It's karaoke.

I can't read, I told her.

She laughed. I hadn't meant it as a joke; I'd meant it as
a lie. Anyway, she dropped trying to persuade me.

We drank rum and cokes. Lara made friends with
various men in the audience. She introduced me to some
of them over the music. I'd nod briefly and then stand
in silence, pretending to be interested in whoever was
performing. I could feel the nervousness in my collar-
bones, the insides of my neck.

It wasn't even eleven before Lara leant into my ear
and shouted that she was leaving. She threw her thumb
over her shoulder, gesturing to a student with a rip in
his T-shirt and a dog tag. I lingered for a few minutes
after she left, looking around aimlessly, convinced that
I'd blown it, and then I went home myself.

After that night we saw a lot of each other. Lara would
invite herself around to mine. I'd make her dinner,

usually beans on toast, while she looked up club nights on Facebook. She lived a few blocks away from me, in a house full of computer science students that she'd found online. I never met any of them.

My house is dead, Lara would text. I'm coming over.

After we ate, we'd get ready to go out. Lara liked to dress me up. She told me I suited eyeliner, so I let her draw big flicks on the corners of my eyes. She'd make me wear one of her tiny lace thongs under a pair of her black skinny jeans, with the thong pulled high so you could see it above the waistband. The thong was so uncomfortable I ended up with a rash, and Lara's jeans made me feel like a rodent being squeezed to death by a boa constrictor. I didn't protest. I understood that I was her project.

Lara dragged me along to various clubs, carrying nothing but her driving licence in her bra. Men would buy her drinks, and occasionally they'd buy mine too. I still wasn't good at conversation, but it turned out that I didn't need to be. My new outfits could do the talking. I went out with Lara night after night, staying far later than I could reasonably handle. I'd exhaust myself into oblivion, then spend the daytime swallowing down ill-advised doses of paracetamol, entire bottles of Lucozade.

It really was a whole new world: music so heavy I could feel it in my ankles, pills that stole hours. I did a lot of squatting on the floors of smoking areas, Lara blowing rings. I don't know if I was enjoying myself or just in a continual state of curiosity. For the first few months, I felt as if I was gliding through a museum. I once got home in the early hours of the morning – stinking of vodka lemonade, eating a jar of glacé cherries I'd bought from the newsagents on my walk back – just as my housemates were leaving for early lectures. They looked me up and down as we crossed paths in the front garden. I stood with my key in the lock and watched them move towards the bus stop, struck dumb by the nothingness of my old life.

Some nights, I'd study Lara for flashes of ugliness. I'd take note of the strange angle her wrist bent into when she was doing up her fly in the toilet cubicle, or the crusty flakes of skin that would build up under her lipstick when we'd had a long night, or the way her pupils would roll back in her head on the dance floor, as if she were searching for something inside her mind. I liked these moments; they made me feel closer to her.

Lara's beauty elevated her above the rest of us. She could pick up things she wanted like dominoes, and scatter the rest. I'm freezing, she said once, to a kind-eyed stoner wearing one of the nicest Carhartt canvas jackets I've ever seen. We were standing in a queue outside a club. The boy shouldered his jacket off and passed it to Lara.

Give it back once we're inside, yeah? he said. It was a Christmas present from my mum. She'll kill me if I lose it.

As soon as the boy's back was turned, Lara pulled me by the wrist. We sloped away, her zipping up her new jacket against the night.

Another time, a few weeks after this, Lara was sitting on a barstool in the Queen's Head, drinking a pint. A group of schoolgirls were dancing on the pool table, playing Ariana Grande out of their phones. Mark was lingering nearby.

I met that guy with the ponytail in the petrol station, she said.

I hadn't seen him since the night Lara and I first met. What were you doing in there? I asked. You don't even have a car.

I wanted to see if I could coax whoever was working out of their shift.

Why?

Something to do.

I didn't say anything to Lara then.

Didn't you notice the Shell logo on his T-shirt? she asked.

I shrugged. I hadn't. What did you say to him? I said.

I just asked if he fancied a game of pool. He left the counter empty and we walked over here. Lara laughed.

D'you think he got fired?

She contemplated the idea. Probably, she said.

I knew that she hadn't actively been trying to get him out of a job. Lara wasn't malicious like that. She'd just wanted someone to fuck, and there he was.

The first time Lara kissed me, we'd just been kicked out a bar. We were wearing matching mesh tops that you could see our nipples through. I looked appalling, and Lara looked great. She'd been caught in the beer garden with a bottle of Amaretto she'd smuggled in under her jacket. I'd told the bouncer it was mine, and we'd both been made to leave. There was a fight going on in the street outside. I'd never seen a proper fight before, not up close like that. I had to watch in snatches, through my fingers. One man grabbed the other's face and pulled it towards him so the two men were standing nose to nose. He didn't take his hand away, and I could see the skin of the other man's cheek stretched tight over his jawbone. Blood and saliva were dripping from inside his mouth.

Lara was excited. Whose side are you on? she asked me.

I don't know, neither. The police will be here in a minute.

I like the one with the tattoo, she said. He's got the edge.

We stood with the rest of a small crowd to watch. The fight looked equal to me. One second one man was under the other, scraping against the tarmac, and the next they'd swapped places. Finally, the man with the tattoo pushed the other very hard into a car. The windscreen cracked against his head and he slid to the ground.

Told you, Lara said.

The winner dusted his hands off on his jeans, as if he'd just finished rolling out pastry. The crowd began to disperse. It was then that Lara put her hands on either side of my face and leant in. Her mouth was molten and luscious. I closed my eyes. Her hand tugged casually at my hair. I could hear the music playing in the bar, and the occasional whoosh of passing traffic. I didn't question the kissing. I just kept doing it. It was nice. When Lara pulled away, the winner of the fight was looking at us. He had his arms folded across his chest, and he was smirking. Lara nodded at him.

Hey, she said.

He nodded back. Hey.

I glanced down at the loser's bloodied face on the pavement. He appeared serene, as if sleeping, surrounded by a fine glitter of glass. Someone was knelt down next to him, trying to rouse him awake. I looked at Lara, looking at the winner, and I understood. I said my goodbyes, bought myself a portion of chips with curry sauce, and walked home through the black streets.

◆

Lara and I had been friends about two months when I went home for Easter.

You look thin, my mother said, the night I arrived. Are you eating properly?

I've been dieting, I lied.

The real reason I'd lost weight was because I spent most days sleeping, and by the time I got up again it was almost time for another night out. There wasn't much opportunity for meals.

My mother looked proud. You must tell me what you do, she said. I'm in a rut with the Atkins.

It's just cucumber, I said. There's no secret.

I slept around fourteen hours that night, and sixteen the next. For the rest of my trip, I averaged around twelve. I must have really needed it. Most days, I was still exhausted. I could barely keep my eyes open long enough to watch an episode of *Peep Show*.

My father kept inviting me to do various activities with him. He'd retired the year I went to university, and I think he was bored at home alone with my mother. He did tennis lessons on Wednesdays, and he'd bought a little rowboat to go fishing on the river. I always liked spending time with my father, but that Easter I didn't take him up on his offers. I wasn't in the mood to be active, and I had tons of work to be getting on with. Since meeting Lara, my grades had slipped so monumentally that I was starting to receive threatening emails. I hadn't been to a lecture in weeks.

By the end of the holidays, I'd made some headway with catching up on assignments, and my energy levels were refreshed. It was good to feel normal, if a little boring. By now I knew what I was missing. As I sat on the train back to the city, I composed six or seven different text messages to Lara. I didn't send a single one.

From the station, I went straight to the Queen's Head to check the rota. It was late. The pub was empty apart from Quaver, who was collecting up the coasters. He came over to me, wiping his hands on his jeans. Since the Christmas holidays, he'd changed his hair from yellow to turquoise, and had two new face piercings.

Those schoolgirls left some open J2Os here that haven't been touched, he said. D'you fancy one? I could put some gin in.

Sure, I said.

Quaver had never shown any interest in me before. I was wearing one of Lara's jackets, and I must've been looking good. We sat at the bar together to drink. Quaver did most of the talking. He was studying agriculture. He wanted to grow vegetables. Leeks are so beautiful, he said.

I didn't really get him. He asked me what I wanted to do, and I told him that bar work suited me fine.

Next time you make a stir-fry, he said, try adding a spoonful of peanut butter.

I'd never made a stir-fry before, but I promised him I'd try it.

We stayed up late drinking. I worried that Mark would catch us, but Quaver didn't seem bothered. I figured if we were going down, we were going down together.

Eventually, I invited Quaver back to mine. There was something about him that made me feel bold. I'd only slept with one other person before, under a hedge in the front garden of a house party when I was fifteen. I hadn't enjoyed it, and had been avoiding sex ever since. With Quaver, it was OK. The skin on his palms was rough as wood. He had coarse stubble, but his shaved, dyed head felt like carpet. I wouldn't call the experience pleasurable, but I appreciated his textures.

The next morning, Quaver was gone before I woke up. Lara came over at around midday. She looked rough. There was none of the ceremony that I'd been hoping for. I wondered if she'd even noticed that I'd been gone. I wiped her face with a hot cloth and made her a sandwich. She fell asleep on my bed and I sat on the floor for five hours watching YouTube videos with my headphones on, so as not to disturb her. When she woke up, we went to the kitchen together. I made her another sandwich while she smoked rollies at the table. One of my housemates came in for a baked potato. She had the worst eczema of all of them, and every time she moved a few flakes of her skin floated to the floor.

Can you not smoke inside, she said.

Lara didn't react, and my housemate looked at me. Meg, she said.

It's fine, I mumbled, and went to crack a window.

That night we were going to a warehouse party. Back in my bedroom, Lara pulled a PVC dress out her bag and told me to put it on. I'd gained back a few pounds, from eating properly over Easter, and I looked like a deflated balloon. We drank cheap white wine. Lara worked mascara into her eyelashes in thick layers.

I had sex last night, I announced.

Oh yeah, she said. With who? She sounded like she didn't believe me.

Quaver. He, um, works in the Queen's Head.

Turquoise hair?

I had a dizzy feeling in my stomach. Yes, I said.

Oh yeah. Had him.

When?

A few weeks ago, while you were away.

Her voice didn't change pitch at all. She was still doing her mascara. I picked up one of her lipsticks and started applying it amateurishly.

You know who else I fucked recently, Lara said.

I held my breath. I didn't want to know.

My mum's ex-boyfriend. I bumped into him in WH Smith. He was up here for some work thing. He told me he barely recognised me, all grown up.

That's gross.

Lara laughed. Isn't it?

The lipstick looked hideous on me. There's lots of men in the world, Lara, I said.

Our eyes met in the mirror. Lara looked almost shocked for a moment, and then she grinned. I know, she said. Isn't it wonderful?

The warehouse party was held under some disused railway arches, and had a snaking queue organised by metal barriers. Tickets were expensive, but Lara knew someone on the door. Inside, the lights were low and flashing. I followed Lara into a huge crowd, collecting other people's sweat on my arms as I elbowed past. Everyone was drinking tap water from tiny plastic cups, and had ringing, orb-like pupils. In the centre of the crowd, I danced to a beat that didn't change for hours, and Lara stuck her tongue in so many mouths I gave up keeping track.

At around 3 a.m., Lara took my hand and dragged me to the square of portaloos that were serving as bathrooms. There was a single hose coming out one of the walls and people were using it to wash their hands. A man had come with us from the dance floor, and Lara introduced him to me as Stevie. He had a bald, waxy head and shifting eyes. He seemed like he was waiting for something. We stood chatting for a while. He kept mentioning his daughter, a seven-year-old called Princess. She was fussy with her food, and Stevie found it hard to get her to eat anything but Milkybars.

I said I needed a wee, although I didn't, and went and locked myself in a portaloo. Pretty soon, there was a knock.

Meg?

It was Lara. I let her in. The cubicle stank of piss and was much too small for the both of us. She looked a bit out of it, and was smiling at me guiltily. She asked me if I wanted some coke. Sure, I said.

I was still finding my footing with drugs. An online forum had advised me to take a little, and wait an hour to see how I felt before taking a little more. So far, this technique had been working fine.

OK great, said Lara. Stevie's got it. He's a dealer, I think.

Are you saying you want some money? I was completely sincere.

No, no, that's the fun bit, Lara said. He wants a blow job.

Lara used a piece of toilet paper to polish her scratched-up reflection in the portaloo mirror. She was deadly serious; I could tell by the way she was looking at herself.

Why can't you do it, I said.

Oh, come on. I got us in here free. You're wearing my dress. I do everything, Meg.

She said that last sentence slowly, her eyes on mine through the mirror. Then she pushed the plastic door open and left me in there. I waited, and when Stevie knocked, I let him in.

I woke up the next day with huge blanks in my memory, and a taste in my mouth like liquorice. I pulled the duvet up over my head and stayed in the dark heat for ages, refusing to open my eyes. It took a long time to persuade myself to confront the world. When I finally did, I found that Lara was sitting on the end of my bed. She looked radiant in the afternoon sunlight coming in through my window. She handed me a carton of orange juice, fresh from the supermarket fridge, and a pot of strawberry yoghurt. Lara had never bought me anything before. I downed most of the juice, and peeled the lid off the yoghurt.

Good morning, she said.

That was all it took.

◆

Term started again that Monday. I didn't go, and neither did Lara. Twelve minutes after our first lecture was due to start, we each received an email. Lara had been officially expelled from the course. I had this term to prove myself, or I would follow suit. Lara seemed dispirited by the news. As for me, I was pleased that they'd even noticed my absence.

Lara picked a bottle of whisky from the off-licence, which I paid for, and we went and got drunk in the park. It was raining heavily, so we sat under a large tree. Its new spring leaves were fluorescent against the white sky. My jeans got damp from the spongy ground and seeped through to my knickers. I'd never got drunk in a park before. It wasn't even midday.

I wonder if people think we're homeless, I mused.

Probably, said Lara. Anyway, I will be soon. No student loan means no rent.

I pressed my hands between my thighs to warm them. Would your mum help, I asked. Just until you find a job.

Lara laughed sourly. Would she fuck.

I drank some more of the whisky. Things were drowsy and nice. Come and live with me, I said.

Mm, said Lara. She was picking at her hangnails, subdued.

We were silent for ages. This was the closest to emotional I'd seen Lara get. Until that point, I'd never had any idea how she was feeling. I started spewing words just to fill the silence. You'll be in much less debt than the rest of us, I said. Degrees are useless anyway, everyone knows. I could get you a job at the Queen's Head, if you want.

Lara didn't respond.

Yeah, I said. The pay's shit, and those schoolgirls squeal like brakes that need oiling. You could do better.

Desperate, I started talking about the weather. The rain, I said. It's not so bad, really. The sounds it makes when it hits the—

Meg, give it a fucking rest.

I looked out onto the wet park, holding my breath. I was tired and drunk, and my hands had started quivering. I stood up, dusted my jeans off, and walked home in the pouring rain.

The next day, I went to my tutorial. Nice of you to show up, my teacher said, as I walked in.

I apologised profusely, and bit back a smile.

On my way home, I bought Lara a baby rabbit from a scuzzy pet shop. The rabbit had been put outside on the street, asleep in a cage full of sawdust. There was a sign on the cage that read *Lionhead, £12*. I suppose the shopkeeper thought some passer-by would be unable to resist. I was that sucker. I hoped a new pet might cheer Lara up. The rabbit was grey, and its fur was a soft, matted fleece. Underneath, its bones felt shockingly fine. The shopkeeper couldn't tell me if it was a boy or a girl, but I knew already.

Lara seemed pleased with him. I hadn't got a cage or anything, so we just let him hop around her room while she packed up her stuff. Every so often, we'd lose him under the bed, and have to coax him out with a leaf of iceberg. I asked Lara what she wanted to call him.

Doug, she said, without a pause.

Doug, like Douglas?

Doug like Meg. Something about him reminds me of you.

I smiled goofily, flushed with pride.

That evening, I helped Lara move into my bedroom. We walked the four blocks between our houses five times, lugging cardboard boxes along with us. After, I called in sick to my shift. On the phone, Mark sounded dubious. I didn't care; he could fire me if he wanted. It was only nine o'clock, but I got into my single bed with Lara and we lay there listening to the faint, methodical thumps of Doug exploring the carpet.

Night, Lara said. Thanks, by the way.

Night.

Lara fell asleep quickly. I could tell by her breathing. She was lying on her side, facing towards me. I turned on my side too, so that our noses were almost touching. I lay there for a long time, trying to breathe in the same air that she breathed out. It was hot as the inside of her body must have been, and it tasted of petrol.

◆

Living with Lara was as I had imagined. My bedroom became a lawless nest of fishnets, dirty underwear, rotting carrot sticks. Lara would do things like fall asleep with a half-drunk bottle of fruit cider balanced in the duvet, and we'd wake up stinking of it, our forearms stuck to each other. She'd sit on the floor and trim her fringe, tiny pieces of hair fluttering around her that I'd have to fish out of my tea for weeks after. Once, I got the hoover out as a hint and left it in the doorway while I went to my lectures. Lara managed to overheat it, somehow, and the bag exploded. When I got back, there was black fluff strewn all over the bedroom. It stayed that way for days. I started to feel that it was Lara's room, and to tidy up would be somehow rude. As for Doug, he ate through all my chargers and shredded the entire textbook for my course. Often, he would escape into the rest of the house and wreak havoc in someone else's bedroom. It didn't matter; all of my housemates had stopped speaking to me anyway. The week Lara first moved in, she'd flirted outrageously with two of their boyfriends, and ate the last slice of a birthday cake that one of their grandmothers had baked them.

I'd never been happier. I'd come home from work and make us dinner in the middle of the night, while she painted her nails and tried to find boys she'd slept with on Instagram. For the first time in my life, I had a companion. I suddenly understood why people chose to get married. I loved sharing a bed with her. I'd close my eyes, and when I opened them again it would be morning, as if I had simply blinked, and yet I'd feel perfectly rested.

Other nights, Lara would go out drinking and not come back, and I'd lay awake worrying about what she was getting up to, and with whom. I'd stopped going out much at all by then. I told myself that this was because I was determined to keep my place at university, when really Lara had stopped inviting me. When she'd finally crash through the door in the early hours of the morning, I'd feel such euphoric relief that my sleepless night was somehow made worth it. We'd curl up together and doze into the afternoon.

Lara had been living with me for around six weeks when she found out her mother was ill. She came into the Queen's Head to tell me. I was useless. I got out from behind the bar and gave her a wooden hug that I regretted instantly. I'm so sorry, I said, as if I was a stranger who'd just bumped into her in the street.

Lara's mother, Tracy, had complained to her doctor of feeling more tired than usual, and shortly afterwards been diagnosed with a cancer that had already taken hold of most of her body. We went down to Norwich on the train. Lara lost her ticket, and I had to buy her another from the conductor. It was nice weather, and we spent the journey in silence, watching the conveyor-belt countryside slip by in the big window.

The hospice had an air of faked warmth. The nurses' footsteps clacked against the wood laminate flooring, and the biscuit tin was empty but for a few sharp little drawing pins. Tracy was sharing a room with a woman attached to a drip. The woman was watching *Antiques Roadshow* so intently that she didn't even blink when we arrived. The television was a tiny box attached to the wall, of the sort I'd only ever seen at car boot sales. Tracy was asleep in a hospital bed under a scratchy sheet, wearing a thick smear of bright pink lipstick.

Lara had bought a cone of yellow roses at the station, which she lay down on the bedside table. The paper crackled, and then there was quiet. Lara and I stood awkwardly, not looking at each other. I watched Tracy's chest, trying to ascertain if she was breathing. A good few minutes passed before she spoke.

Get rid of those, she said. It's the smell. Can't think. Makes me want to vomit.

She still didn't open her eyes. Her face was grey and sunken. I realised she hadn't been asleep at all. Lara picked the flowers back up and tossed them in the wastepaper basket in the corner. Sorry, she said.

Why didn't you come sooner?

Lara apologised again. I reached for her hand but she pulled away.

Tracy opened her eyes, looked us both over and scoffed. Nice outfit, she said. Appropriate.

I thought of my own mother, who stocked up on my favourite herbal teas when I went home. I introduced myself, and Tracy frowned at me blankly.

You could've at least called, Tracy said to Lara.

I—

Every day, the nurses ask me when my daughter's coming. Tomorrow, I tell them.

Mum, I—

Tracy's voice was a little raspy. Rhea's daughter comes in the mornings before work, she said. Brings pastries. After work, she brings her little son. Charmer. Yesterday, he gave Rhea that balloon.

Lara and I both looked at the woman in the other bed. There was a heart-shaped balloon attached to her drip. Rhea nodded at us, then returned her gaze to the television.

That's lovely, I said.

Tracy closed her eyes again. Her chest started going up and down very fast.

We should go, Lara said.

I looked at the cone of roses in the bin. We only just got here.

Lara's voice hardened. Meg, she said.

Out the window, the sun slid behind a cloud, and the room became three shades darker. Through the gap in the door, I watched a nurse push an empty wheelchair down the corridor. On *Antiques Roadshow*, a café owner was told that his grandmother's vase was worthless. Lara turned to leave, and I looked one last time at Tracy. Her eyebrows drew together a little, and then her eyelids flickered. I willed her to open them. She didn't.

Lara and I caught the bus back to the station, where we sat on hard plastic seats for three hours, drinking bad filter coffee and watching the announcement board light up with trains going all over the country.

Lara spent the entire journey back doing her make-up, using the black screen of my smartphone as a mirror. She drank a dented can of pre-mixed sangria that she found at the bottom of her backpack. She didn't offer me any. When we got to the city, Lara walked with me down to the bus stop, but when our bus arrived she didn't get on.

I'm going out, she said.

I didn't ask where she was going. I doubt she even knew. It was five o'clock on a Tuesday afternoon, but she'd find somewhere. I sat at the back of the bus and watched her silhouette get smaller and smaller. It was drizzling, and the street lights bled in the windows.

Later, alone in my bedroom, I looked up a set of earrings online. They were hoops with a pair of red diamante lips suspended in the middle by a slinky gold chain. Months before, I'd seen those earrings in the shopping section of a magazine that one of my housemates had left in the kitchen, and they'd reminded me instantly of Lara. I couldn't remember the name of the magazine, or the brand of the earrings, so I just typed the description of them into Google. I wanted to give Lara a present to show her I was there for her. The earrings were two hundred pounds, far more than I'd ever spent on a single purchase. I entered my card details and ordered them.

Lara didn't come home that night. I waited in for her all the next day, half-listening to the recorded lectures that my teachers uploaded to the student portal. For lunch I made a stir-fry with peanut butter and fed some of it to Doug. When I went to the Queen's Head for my shift at five thirty, Lara was in there, passed out across the pool table. The schoolgirls were huddled around her, gripping their bottles of Bacardi Breezer so tight I could see the bone through their knuckles.

I charged through the crowd. Out my way, I said.

One of the schoolgirls put her hand on my elbow and looked at me very seriously. I think she might be dead, she said.

I brushed the hand away. She's fine. She's just tired.

I slipped one arm under Lara's neck and the other under her knees. Lara's head fell back as I lifted her, and her mouth opened. Her tongue was covered with a layer of thick, yellow scum. The schoolgirls gasped.

Mark, I called. You'll have to cover me. I'll be back in half an hour.

Sure, said Mark. He moved into the crowd, resting his hands on a couple of the schoolgirls' waists. As I carried Lara outside, I could hear him speaking to them in soft tones. You poor little things, he said. Let's have another drinky, make it all better.

Lara was heavier than I thought she'd be. I kept having to stop for breathers on the walk home, laying her body down on a low hedge or the thin red bench inside the bus shelter. She didn't seem to notice. The only sound she made was a light, wheezy snore whenever I picked her up or put her down. Back at the house, I couldn't reach around to get my key out my pocket, so I knocked on the front door and waited for one of my housemates to answer.

Jesus, said my housemate. It was the one with the psoriasis. Has there been an accident?

Of sorts, I said.

Does she need an ambulance?

I shook my head. She just needs to sleep it off.

I carried Lara through the doorway, and at the bottom of the stairs I stopped and looked back at my housemate. Would you mind? I said.

My housemate took Lara under the armpits and together we carried her up the stairs. I was embarrassed when I opened my bedroom, because of the state of it. By this point, Doug's droppings had started to break down to a dark fuzz that became part of the carpet. If Lara and I walked barefoot in there, the fresher ones would stick to the soles of our feet like flattened raisins. The smell though, I think, was coming mostly from the piss. It was putrid and tangy. Once, I left a textbook for one of my modules on the floor for a few days, and when I picked it up again the paper was crinkled, dark yellow from cover to cover.

We hauled Lara onto the bed. My housemate retreated to the doorway and lingered there, looking on, while I carefully removed Lara's boots and jewellery. I picked up Doug from the floor and tucked him into the covers to keep Lara company. I leant down and gave them both a kiss on the forehead, one after the other.

Are you guys, like, a thing now? my housemate asked, as I closed the bedroom door behind us.

You mean me and Lara? I gave a tiny laugh. No way.

After my shift was over, I went via the supermarket to pick up some supplies. I figured Lara would need a good meal, and I bought some Berocca tablets and a bag of oranges, for the vitamins. They were selling daffodils at the checkout for cheap. I picked up a bunch.

It was dark out, and the sky was murky from the street lights. My body was sore from carrying Lara and work-ing an eight-hour shift. I didn't have a bag, so I held my shopping wrapped in my arms. As I walked, I thought about asking Lara to give me a massage. She'd sit with all her weight on my bum, and rub her hands up and down my back. I closed my eyes for a few steps while I pictured this, and then I tripped over a kerb and landed funny on my ankle. I was fine, but my shopping was everywhere.

I was gonna do eggs, I said, as I pushed my bedroom door open. But I smashed them all, so it's just cheese on—

I'd gone straight to the kitchen when I got in. I was hungry, and I assumed Lara would be too. She'd probably not eaten for over twenty-four hours by this point. I'd filled a tray with the plates, two fizzing glasses of Berocca, and a water jar for the daffodils. I had to walk into the room backwards, because I had no hands to get the door open. When I turned around, Lara was naked on my bed, sitting upright with her face towards the window and a man between her legs.

I dropped the tray on the floor. The toast landed cheese-side down. The Berocca dyed a large patch of the carpet coral.

Sorry, I said. Shit, sorry.

Lara looked over her bare shoulder, as if seeing what it was that I wanted.

Sorry, I said again. I rushed out the room, kicking the tray aside to let the door close behind me. I stood with my back pressed against it, feeling the sobs rise up in my chest. It wasn't long before the man came out. He was pulling his arm through a bright red fleece, and he had a large red satchel slung over his opposite shoulder. The bag was gaping open, and inside were hundreds of envelopes.

Are you a fucking postman? I said.

The man Velcro-ed his bag shut. Nah, he said. I just wear this outfit for kicks.

He started to make his way down the corridor, dragging his feet as he walked. At the top of the stairs, something occurred to him, and he turned around and came back. I thought he was going to apologise, but instead he dipped into his bag and handed me a small package.

Thanks, I said. I shook the package gently. Inside, Lara's earrings jangled.

The man nodded. Uh huh, he said.

◆

The day after, I was buying a Twix in a newsagent when my card got declined. I checked online banking on my phone, and found that I only had thirty-four pence in my account. The man behind the counter slid the Twix away from me slowly, as if it was some kind of weapon I'd been brandishing.

When I got home, Lara was sitting on the bed, stroking Doug's ears. The daffodils, still strewn across the floor, had withered in the night. I noticed that Doug had tried to eat one and then changed his mind.

Lara and I hadn't spoken about the postman. I'd slept on the sofa, and when I'd come in that morning to change, Lara was still asleep. Now she was drinking a Fosters out of a reusable Starbucks cup. I knew it was a Fosters because I could see the empty can on the floor next to her. That Starbucks cup was one of my housemate's most prized possessions. Lara must have stolen it from the kitchen.

All my money's gone, I said.

Huh?

There's no money in my bank account.

Lara took a sip from the cup. It was translucent pink, with a plastic screw-on lid and a straw coming out the top. Drinking a lager out of it looked obscene.

Have you been spending my money? I asked.

Lara put her head to one side. A bit.

I was surprised at how nonchalantly she was admitting it. I asked her what she'd been spending it on. I knew that this wasn't important, in the scheme of things, but I wanted to know.

Taxis, she said. Drugs. She looked around the room, disinterested. I just take your card out with me sometimes, she said.

You take my card while I'm asleep?

Lara nodded. It's not like you're using it.

In spite of myself, I laughed. It was like being a parent of a small, unusually witty child. They drive you crazy, and yet you love them. Lara laughed too, and then got up off the bed and put her arm around me. She was still holding Doug in her other hand, and his whiskers tickled my neck.

You spent my entire student loan for this semester, I said. I wanted to sound annoyed, but it came out half-hearted.

I know.

This was the closest I got to an apology. Lara stayed hugging me for some time, Doug nestled between us, and eventually I gave in and hugged her back. As I did, I reasoned with myself that I could borrow the money for the next two months' rent, interest-free, from my father, who might even forget about it. Lara didn't have anyone to ask that. As for the Twix, I didn't even want it anymore.

Lara, I said. The skin of her shoulder was cool against my cheek. Maybe you should take some time out for a bit, just try and slow down.

Lara's body stiffened. She pulled away from me. She threw Doug to the floor. He froze when he hit the carpet, and I flinched. I bent down to get him, but before I could he'd shuffled under the bed to hide.

Who do you think you are, Meg? My mother?

I got back up, shaking my head. My lips opened but no words came out. I closed them again. I didn't want to cry in front of Lara, but I was.

Fuck this, Lara said.

The bedroom door shook the whole house as it slammed, and the front door did the same.

Please, shouted one of my housemates. I'm trying to study.

◆

Lara wasn't back the next day, or the one after, or the one after that. Every time I called, her phone went straight to answer machine. Whenever one of my housemates got home, I ran to the top of the stairs to see who it was.

I tried to go about my life in an ordinary fashion. I attended my lectures and went to the library, where I mostly just sat with a book open on the desk and scrolled through photos of Lara on my phone until it was time for my shift at the Queen's Head, where I stood behind the bar and did the same.

At the weekend, I cried for three hours, and then I cleaned my bedroom from top to bottom. It took me a day and a half. Doug watched with great interest, twitching his nose.

I went to the post office on Monday morning. I hadn't even opened the package before I returned it. On my way home I stood at the crossing of a busy junction for twelve minutes, waiting for the lights to change. There was an old man with a stick standing next to me. If you ever want to kill yourself, he said, this is the place to do it.

I turned to him. His skin was sunken and translucent. I could see the green veins in his neck, the shape his eye sockets would be in the grave. I thought of Lara, the most alive person I'd ever known. Thanks for the tip, I said.

That evening, one of my housemates asked me if Lara had moved. We were in the kitchen, wordlessly fixing ourselves separate meals. When I told her no, Lara had simply gone out and not come back, she was alarmed. Call the police, she said, picking nervously at a cold sore on the edge of her mouth. For god's sake, anything could have happened.

I thought of a police car cruising around, slowing to check for Lara in various ditches and alleyways. A part of me wished that she had been murdered, just so I could get on with my life.

Six days after she left, Lara came back. I answered the door at four o'clock in the morning and there she was, scuffing the toe of her big black boot against the front step. She looked dreadful. The whites of her eyes were the colour of salmon, and there was a huge hole in one knee of her fishnets; a raw, seeping graze in the middle of it.

That's it, she said. She's gone.

For a moment, I thought Lara had died after all, and this was her ghost, referring to itself in the third person, returned to haunt me. I was struck by catastrophic grief, and then I put my finger on it. Your mother, I said.

Obviously, Meg.

Are you feeling OK?

Lara puffed her cheeks at me and pushed her way in. She went straight upstairs. I made her a decaf coffee in the kitchen and spiked it with rum. When I got to the bedroom, Lara was sitting on the edge of the bed, Doug dozing in her lap. I wondered if he'd missed her as much as I had.

Looks tidy in here.

Thanks, I said. It's easier without, you know—

Me.

That's not what I meant.

There was silence for a while. Are you staying, I asked.

Do you want me to?

Of course I want you to.

I sat tentatively next to Lara on the bed and fought the desire to ask her where she'd been. It seemed the only option was to love her while she was here, and just try to scrape through the times when she wasn't.

I bought this. It's for Doug.

She was holding up a bag of watercress. The leaves were slightly darker than normal, and had leaked a vivid green liquid into one corner of the bag. I ripped it open and emptied the contents into a cereal bowl that I kept on the floor for rabbit pellets.

Lara went to brush her teeth. When she came back, she looked pale and sad. She took all her clothes off, got into bed and turned to face the wall. Doug finished his meal, balled up inside the bowl and closed his eyes. I found a recording of whale song on YouTube, pressed play on my phone, and climbed in next to Lara.

What the fuck is this?

I thought it might help you sleep, I whispered.

She rolled over, and I could feel her breath hot on my face. She put her mouth on mine. Her tongue tasted like mint imperials. I listened to the whales moaning. The kissing seemed to go on forever. It was slow and beautiful, and then Lara was stroking my stomach and kissing other parts of my body. I looked at the ceiling and tried to focus.

Lara, I said. Are you sure?

Lara found my hand under the duvet and brought it between her legs. Her skin was cool and slinky as nylon tights, and I closed my eyes because I couldn't stand the burning sight of her.

Shut up, she whispered.

She lifted my pyjamas off. I could feel the pulse in my clitoris, and then my nipples, my toenails, and finally in the hair follicles all over my head. Out the window, the sun was just rising. The sky was the palest blue, with tiny strokes of fire. A bird in a nearby tree hooted. I came, and then I tried to make Lara come, and failed.

I apologised.

It's fine, she said. You were better than I expected.

Really?

Don't push it, Meg.

I fell straight to sleep after that. Lara's hair was tangled in my hand. I didn't dream. I woke smiling. The whale song had cut out, and Lara was gone. This time, she'd taken all her stuff with her. I searched the room for Doug, calling his name frantically. I pulled everything out from under the bed. I turned his cereal bowl upside down. I was lying face down on the carpet when I heard him scrabbling at the wardrobe door. Lara must have shut him in there by accident when she packed her clothes. I opened the wardrobe. Doug looked up at me, twitched his nose, and hopped out into the light.

Send Nudes

In a bus stop, she listens as two people discuss an approaching storm.

Worst in fifty years. Worst in my lifetime.

Not in mine. I was a kid, I remember it. The river flooded. Boats were sailing down the streets instead of cars.

Oh, this one'll flood the river. For sure it'll flood the river.

It's good, she thinks, to hear voices at rush hour. It doesn't happen often. A bus pulls into the stop, and one of the people engaged in the conversation gets on. The other stays behind. He's wearing a blue anorak. She's standing next to him, close enough to continue his conversation. She too knows about the storm. She's seen it on the news, a red blur sliding across the Atlantic.

She doesn't say anything. She watches her reflection in the black windows of passing traffic. She watches the reflections of the commuters around her. There are ten or twelve people, all wearing wireless earphones, standing close enough that she could reach out and touch them. Their reflections are bleary in the glass. When the traffic lurches, the reflections lurch. Soon, she has motion sickness from watching. The arm of the man in the blue anorak brushes against her.

I don't feel well, she could say. I need a hand.

She looks at the concrete sky, at the concrete ground. The sickness passes. Another bus pulls into the stop, the man with the blue anorak steps on. After him, more people push to board. She can hear the travel cards bleep as they're scanned. Through the bus window, she can see the man sitting on a seat, staring at his hands.

Bye, she could have said.

She feels around in her handbag for her phone. She checks that no one's watching, and then she opens an app. She downloaded the app this afternoon, in her lunch break. It works by matching two anonymous strangers from anywhere in the world, for a conversation in messages.

When she opens the app, her heart rises up her throat like acid reflux. She swears she can hear it beating. She

looks back over her shoulder. The commuters are staring ahead. They cannot hear her heart because of their
wireless earphones. Her own wireless earphones are
broken.

In the app, she types a greeting, then deletes it. Her
heart is so loud and fast she's struggling to think. She
types another greeting, deletes it again. This happens
twice more. The beating is louder still. She cannot focus.
She feels frantic. Every beat makes her left eye wink
involuntary. She closes her eyes for a long time. Then
she opens them again, swallows her heart back down,
presses send.

hello

The message sounded better in her head. Simple,
she'd thought. Classic. For thirty seconds, she receives
no reply. The message is a disused plastic bag riding a
breeze, skimming the pavement.

asl?

She blinks. A frown passes over her eyebrows. *sorry?*
this is my first time.

age sex location

excuse me?

it stands for age sex location

38 female UK

29 male UK

where in the UK?

London

what are the odds?

describe urself

Ah, she thinks. Ah ha. She looks down at herself. *curvy. brunette.*

It's fair to say that some adjectives sound better than others. Using the better adjectives is only a little white lie, like wearing shapewear, or having lowlights put in at the salon.

what u wearing?

She is wearing a black A-line dress, 80 denier tights, and shapewear in two sizes too small. The shapewear restricts her breathing, makes her feel hot at all times, takes three inches off her waist.

lingerie. red.

These are no longer white lies, but lying comes with the territory. Two people don't sit on either side of a screen rather than either side of a coffee table if they're going to be completely honest about themselves. She could be ninety-five years old. She could be missing three fingers on one hand. She could be officially cate-gorised as obese, in terms of BMI. The stranger wants to imagine a certain type of woman, and she will let him.

where r u?

in bed. you?

Another bus pulls into the stop. She puts her phone in her pocket and prepares to board. There are no seats on the bus. She holds a yellow rail for support while she stands in the aisle. When she looks again at her phone, there's another message.

same. pretty horny tbh.

She is aware of her nipples beneath her shapewear. The bus lurches as it starts up, and the side of her hip brushes against a teenage boy in a hoodie.

I want u, writes the stranger.

I want you, she replies.

Outside, fine rain comes down from a faded orange sky and speckles the Perspex windows. The teenage boy with the hoodie opens a packet of Monster Munch. The air smells of pickled onions.

send a pic of ur body.

She smiles. *you first.*

The photograph loads in sections, shifting from pixelated to clear. She holds her phone very close to her face, in the hope that none of the other passengers will catch sight of the screen. And then, there it is: his narrow, hairy body, in the yellow light of what is perhaps a kitchen, his penis hard in his hand. Underneath, one of the stranger's feet can be seen, bare on the beige linoleum. His big toe is long and angular, with a nodule of hard skin protruding outwards at the side, a fuzz of dark hair on the knuckle.

u like what u see?

yes. particularly the toe.

lol thanks

There is silence in the app. Then, *u like my cock?*

She glances over her shoulder. *yes. very nice.*

ur turn. send nudes.

She returns her phone to her bag. For the rest of the journey, she holds the yellow bar softly, stroking it with the pad of her thumb, as if it's the hand of a lover.

The first thing she does after work is go for a run. Sunset is over, the street lights are on. The park behind her building is closed in case any trees come down in the wake of the storm. She runs the streets. During her run, the rain gets harder. It soaks into her nylon clothes, already soaked with her sweat. The cold air hurts the back of her throat, the concrete reverberates through her knee-caps, her phone throbs in the pocket of her leggings. She worries that her phone will get so wet from the rain that it will break. The stranger will be left in the app, naked and waiting.

ur turn. send nudes.

When she returns to her building, the man living in the flat below hers opens the door as she's reaching to put her key in the lock. He's holding a bin bag. She's sodden, panting on the doorstep. She wraps her arms around her body. She's not wearing her shapewear.

You shouldn't be running alone in the dark, he says, without lifting his head.

Thank you, she whispers. It's the first time someone has spoken aloud to her all day.

A storm's coming.

She nods. Her hair is wet against her forehead, slapping like a strip of raw bacon. Yes. I heard that.

He dumps the bin bag on the pavement outside, and goes back into his flat. She lingers outside his closed door for a moment before going upstairs herself.

She turns the shower on. She can hear the sounds of her own breathing bouncing off the bare walls. In the mirror, she notices that her face is a very bright, deep pink, and a green blood vessel has burst on her right cheek. She peels the damp clothes from her body, studies the rank, sweaty lines that they've etched in her skin. She reaches into the shower, feels the temperature of the falling water, climbs in. She washes her hair, her face, all of her over-soft flesh. This is the worst part of her day: having to confront herself like this.

After, she stands in the shower with the taps off for a while, dripping. Once again, she considers the stranger in the chat room, the hard penis and the big toe. She gives him the face of the man in the flat downstairs, and then she takes it away.

It would be easy to take a photograph of her naked body. It would be quick. And what harm could it do?

She closes her eyes, and in her mind she sees every message the stranger would send in reply.

um

sorry but I'm not rly into big girls

kk I'm gonna disconnect

good luck

hope u find someone

It would be like that, she thinks. Kind, but firm. Men had been cruel about her body in the past – plenty of men – but the stranger in the chat room was different, she could tell. The hints at his character had been small but discernible. For example, he'd been chivalrous, sending her a nude of himself before asking for one in return. He was gentle in the way he composed his messages, almost subdued – *pretty horny tbh* – and she believed that he took time over her responses, really read them before replying. He was a listener, she was sure, and a listener was hard to find. The biggest giveaway, of course, was the photograph he'd sent. It sounded stupid, but it was true: she could see his nature in his big toe. How honest it looked, how normal, and yet how intimate.

She only realises she is crying because she can taste the tears on her lips. She climbs out the shower and walks, naked, still dripping, into the kitchen. Outside, the weather has escalated. Rain hammers against the windows like a piece of experimental music, a single siren can be heard screaming in the distance.

She is hungry. All day, she has only eaten a tuna salad, while sitting at her desk, and a flapjack, in the toilet cubicle of the Pret a few blocks from her office.

There's almost no food in the flat. She keeps her cupboards purposefully bare. The only item is a packet of powdered cheese sauce, slotted behind the toaster. She'd spied it there a few times, when she went underneath with a sponge to wipe away crumbs. She didn't buy the cheese sauce herself; it was left behind by the previous tenant. Always, anxiety has stopped her from throwing it out. What about the end of the world? Most nights, she stays up reading about the state of the planet: drinking straws in the nostrils of sea creatures, football fields of forest shredded in seconds, the temperature climbing up and up.

She boils the kettle, rips the corner from the packet of cheese sauce. She empties the powder into a small metal bowl, adds the hot water. The kettle has a problem with limescale. She can see the silt as she stirs. The sauce ends up with a grainy texture, the taste is sort of metallic. Still, she eats it joyously. Eating is always joyous to her. When she's finished, she licks the bowl clean.

It's cold in the flat. The desire to put a dressing gown on has not struck her as it usually does. She is used to hiding her body, even from herself. Now, the small fact that the stranger wants to see it is enough. She walks from room to room naked. For the first time in years, she can bear to.

She goes to the hallway and cranks up the thermostat, and then she stands with her legs pressed against the radiator until the metal is so hot it burns. While she's standing here, she opens the camera on her phone. She flips the viewfinder so she can see herself in the screen. She looks only at her face. Beneath it, her naked body looms, a great mass. She cannot bring herself to lower the camera.

Whenever she closes her eyes and imagines her body, it expands and constricts to the beat of a pulse, moving between very thin, thinner than she has ever been or could be, and then very fat, fatter than those Americans on television, so fat she would have to be lifted from bed by a crane. In turn, she avoids looking directly at her body. She probably would not be able to see it as it is. If she did see it as it is, that could be worse.

Her face, though, is not so bad. The pink colour has drained out of it, the shower has left her skin matte and clear. There is a small fleck of cheese sauce in each corner of her mouth. She takes a photograph of one fleck and then the other. Watching herself in the screen, she licks them from her skin.

Outside the living room window, lightning cuts the sky. The whole city flashes. She goes to the glass and looks out. Above, telephone wires swing in the wind like skipping ropes. Below, a river of murky water sloshes through the gutter, dragging a clump of something soft: a ball of socks, perhaps, or a drowned rat.

She opens her phone again, looks at the message in the app. The stranger is still online. He hasn't given up on her.

ur turn. send nudes.

She takes a deep breath in. *you there?*

yes

this storm's pretty wild.

not as wild as the things I'd do to u

She sends the photographs of the cheese sauce on the corners of her mouth. She stares at the screen, waiting for the stranger's reply. When it doesn't come, she goes back to the kitchen, starts to wash up the metal bowl to distract herself. Suds spit occasionally across her bare stomach. As she places the bowl on the drying rack, her phone pings.

dirty. i'm into it

She can barely breathe. *what took u so long?*

what do u think

Right then, a tremor runs through the flat. Her feet, for a second, leave the floorboards. The aftershocks fade out, vibrating through her bones.

did you feel that?

feel what?

the tremor

no

She looks at the bowl on the drying rack, the empty packet of cheese sauce on the kitchen counter.

send nudes, writes the stranger again.

She takes a long breath and exhales. She picks up the bowl from the drying rack. She presses it against her right nipple until the skin there is shrivelled and hard. After, she moves across to the other. She scrapes her front teeth against the skin of her lips, aggressively, to draw blood into them. She bends one of her legs upwards, using the kitchen counter to support it, and draws her shoulders back. In this position, she opens the camera on her phone. She stretches her arm out in front of her, the phone angled downwards. She taps her thumb, just once, against the button.

She sends the photograph without looking at it first. It appears in the app encased in a blue speech bubble, serene and ordinary as letters. With one final tap, she disconnects. If the stranger had been composing a reply, she will never read it.

In the morning, in fact, the world is not over. The sky has been swept of clouds and the streets washed clean. She takes a detour through the park on her way to the bus stop, where a huge oak has come down. Today, she has decided against her shapewear. She breathes the new air, feels the oxygen pulse madly through her veins. She is eating a pain au raisin from the bakery on the corner, and flakes of pastry collect with each bite in the fold of her cleavage. When she reaches the tree, she stops to look. It flashes its upturned roots at her, gorgeous and brazen in the new sun.

Flying Kite

Our garden was loveliest in the mornings: all dewed bluebells, wind chimes, watery skies. I was sitting in the yurt's doorway, my knees pulled up to my chest, looking out. Behind me, Jara was teaching a yoga class. The baby was three days overdue, and still Jara's flow was sleek. The curious globe of her belly reminded me of a coconut, sloshing with fluid. When I tried to imagine the baby in there, it was an iridescent fish, swimming in loops.

I liked to dip in and out of Jara's class. My favourite part was the end, when everyone lay on their backs with their eyes closed and considered the spiritual energy moving around their body. I'd feel the warm buzz of it in my toes and let it travel along a kind of wire, all the way up to the hair follicles on the top of my head. I didn't notice my spirit in day-to-day life, but in those yoga classes I knew it was there.

My least favourite part of the class was downward dog. My stomach would hang out the bottom of my T-shirt, and I'd feel the breeze on it. I hated being made aware of my own body, which was white and doughy as a hotdog bun; the exact opposite of Jara's. When I first moved here, I broke the hammock that Oak had strung up in the garden. I'd landed on the hard, packed earth, and understood for the first time just how big I was. At eight years old, I'd broken a hammock that grown adults used every day.

My diet changed dramatically when I moved in with Oak and Jara. My mother used to fill our flat with treats out of guilt. I'd eat ridiculous things for dinner: salt and vinegar crisps mashed into pots of yoghurt, still-frozen potato waffles, the heads of jelly snakes. At Oak and Jara's, we lived mostly on grains and tahini. I'd been eating this way for three years, as well as doing yoga every morning, and still my stomach rippled when I sat down and the insides of my thighs rubbed together in the heat. My body didn't know how to occupy any other space but fat.

It was because of the downward dog that I noticed Anthea. Our garden was a sloping hill of long grass, with the yurt at the top. Oak had taught Kite and me to whistle with that grass last summer and now Kite did it all the time, keeping the loudest blades in his pockets until they dried out. Nobody could hear Anthea knocking from the yurt and only I could see her, lingering as I was in the doorway. She was wearing a grey T-shirt under a denim jacket, plimsolls the colour of satsumas. She looked out of place. Almost everyone who visited our house wore wrap skirts and had long hair dyed maroon with henna.

Anthea was Kite's social worker. When Kite was first brought here, the year after me, she visited every two weeks to check on him. That went on for around three months, but I hadn't seen her in the two years since. Now I watched her silently, crouched on the balls of my feet. She knocked again, waited with her hands on her hips, and then attempted a phone call, probably to the temperamental mobile that Oak and Jara shared but never answered.

When Anthea finally turned to leave, I realised I hadn't been breathing. As soon as the gate was closed, I started again. I rejoined the class in celebration. They were standing with their hands touching above their heads like lit candles at a shrine. The sound of the car exhaust was only just audible over the lull of Jara's voice.

After the class finished, it was my job to put everything away. The yurt got damp at night, so the mats had to be rolled up and taken inside, as well as the sheepskin rugs and the incense burner. It took me five trips before this was done. In the past, Jara would have helped, but these days she was busy carrying new life, something far heavier.

Kite's chore was to hand out energy balls to the class. We made these on Sundays from cashew butter and cacao nibs. The class had a soft spot for Kite. He was six years old, springy and gap-toothed. He spent classes delivering cushions to people who needed something soft to place under their knees, or bending himself into impossible shapes. On Kite's birthday, he received presents from two women in the class: an Om symbol threaded onto a red ribbon, and a hand-carved boomerang with a kangaroo painted on it. He wore the Om around his neck every day, but the boomerang was quickly lost in the hedgerow. On my birthday, the class brought nothing.

It was a warm day, so everyone took a long time to leave. Jara brewed a pot of fresh mint tea, and Oak lay out a tie-dye throw for people to sit on. The class passed around a hash pipe and talked about things I didn't understand, like ayahuasca and chemtrails.

Often, Kite and I went off to play in the corner of the garden where our name trees were planted. We'd practise dance routines. I fancied myself as a choreographer. My routines were always full of hip swishing, kiss blowing and slut drops, like on MTV. Oak and Jara had a strict no-screen policy, but I still remembered all the moves from watching at my mum's. She had one of those televisions with built-in legs, and loads of DVDs she'd bought from the car-boot sale. She liked watching MTV the most. She used to say it stopped her thinking.

Kite was a natural dancer, fast and easy, and he knew how to do a backflip off the big tree stump, which always made an impressive end to our routines. He didn't mind doing sexy-girl dance moves. I don't think he knew that's what they were.

The previous year, Oak's mother had visited from New Zealand. She brought me a Barbie, and Kite a pack of Pokémon cards. The Barbie had plastic strips of glitter in her hair, and the tiniest sunglasses I'd ever seen. When I pulled her head off, her neck was just a stump with a hole in it. She had a very slight bum crack but no vagina.

Kite spent days following me around, asking to play with my Barbie. It always caused a fight when I refused, and one of us would end up in tears. Finally Jara gave in and bought him one. That's the first and last piece of plastic I'm ever bringing into this house, she said, when she gave it to him.

Kite's was a Vet Barbie. She wore jodhpurs and had a pink stethoscope around her neck. She came with a model foal, a lamb, two calves, and a plastic bandage that fit around the legs of the animals. For a year, long after I'd grown bored of my own, Kite took Vet Barbie everywhere. He slept with her at night, and sometimes when he ate he used her flat, gummy hands as little spoons to scoop the food into his mouth.

Kite had never been to school. I don't think he'd been around many kids before me. He wasn't to know what things were for girls, and I certainly didn't plan on telling him. I liked having someone to dance my routines with. Sometimes I wondered if he thought that one day his nipples would begin to swell like mine had, or that he'd wake in the morning to find a bloodstain on his mattress, the size and colour of a two-pence piece.

I didn't go off with Kite to dance that day. Instead I went up to Oak and Jara's bedroom and stole their phone out from the top drawer of their dresser. The house was the sort of cottage that gnomes might live in, with a real thatched roof and wood beams striped across the ceilings. It was old and badly looked after. The damp walls were covered over with hanging tapestries, and the rotting windowsills were crowded with seashells and crystals. The stairs creaked, and the floorboards, and every single drawer. Going up there created a whole orchestra of noise, and I was terrified that someone might hear me. I was wearing yoga pants without pockets, so when I got the phone I stuffed it into the gusset of my knickers. It felt cold and alien in there. I had the urge to pee on it.

Around the side of the house, there was a gate that led out to a public wood. Over the past few weeks, Kite and

I had been building a shelter in the hollow of a huge tree. I was stronger than Kite, so I did all the heavy lifting. I spent hours hunting out the perfect log to use as a sofa, tying sticks together with rope to construct a makeshift door. While I sorted these things, Kite kept house. Every day, he swept the dirt floor with a willow branch and lay down a carpet of dry leaves. He'd pick bluebells and arrange them in small bunches around the place, scrape bits of lichen from the bark of the tree.

This wasn't our first shelter, but it was our best. It was in an overgrown corner of the wood, which meant that it hadn't yet been discovered by local kids in the area. Each of our previous shelters was now a teenage hangout, decorated with cigarette butts, ripped sleeping bags, and the sweet, stale smell of old cider.

The wood was in full leaf, the light coming through like bubbles in a fizzy drink. I felt as if I was being watched through them. I tucked the phone carefully into the darkest reaches of the tree's hollow, the place Kite and I referred to as 'the larder' because we thought it sounded old-fashioned. After, my heart felt fast. I ran home.

Sage, shouted Kite, when I got back through the gate. Come look at this!

The yoga class had all gone. Only Jara and Oak were left sitting on the throw. Kite was over by the vegetable patch, something balanced in his palm. I went to him.

It's a strawberry, he said. There's only two. I ate one, so this is for you.

I took it. The strawberry was just-pink, small and hard as a frozen pea. I ate it in one. It tasted like a Tangfastic. I'm not sure they're ready, I said.

Kite shrugged. Too late now, I guess.

I pulled him into a hug. He seemed surprised; usually it was Jara who did awkward, affectionate things. His skin felt cool against mine. I was still panting from the run. He tried to wriggle out of my arms, but I held on. I spoke into his grubby, matted hair. I've got you, I said.

For lunch we ate seed crackers made in the dehydrator, wild garlic houmous, spiced marrow from the garden, and cold, anaemic blocks of tofu. Jara made us laugh by using her belly as a table on which to balance her bowl. When she took it off, Oak put his hands on her to feel for kicks. The way Oak touched Jara's pregnant belly reminded me of when he played his drum. It was a round steel one, and he hit it very gently with the ends of his fingers to make sounds like lots of tiny frogs jumping into a pond.

Jara had asked Kite and me if we wanted to be at the birth. She thought it was important for us to see how we came into the world. She was planning to have the baby at home. There was an inflatable pool blown up in the living room. When the pool first arrived, Oak filled it with cold water from the hose, and then hot water from the kettle, and we got inside and pretended it was a hot tub. Oak, Jara and Kite all got in naked, but I kept my knickers on. My chest had started to puff up into something like breasts. Floating on top of the water, they resembled the white bellies of two dead fish.

Later that evening, I asked Jara to buy me some training bras next time she went into town. Jara never wore a bra, but that felt different. Her breasts were perfectly symmetrical handfuls with upturned, chestnut nipples.

Sage, you must never be ashamed of your body.

I nodded. Admitting that I was ashamed seemed the most shameful thing I could do.

The training bras Jara bought cut into my armpits, and became stained with greenish patches from my sweat. I left one on the floor of our bedroom once, and found Kite using it as a makeshift hammock for Vet Barbie.

Will the baby be able to choose its own name, Kite asked now. Like me and Sage?

We'd finished lunch, and Oak was washing the dishes. No, he said. This time, we get to choose the baby's name.

Why?

Oak didn't answer.

Isn't it time for lessons? Jara said, and Kite and I went into the cabinet for our schoolbooks.

When Kite first arrived here, his name was Ben. At his naming ceremony, Oak dug a hole next to my tree and planted a sapling. What would you like your new name to be? he asked.

Ben looked around nervously. Kite, he said. The name seemed to come to him at random.

That's beautiful, said Jara. So free.

We held scraps of cloth to our mouths and whispered wishes into them. I wished for Kite to be happy here, and for my mother not to have forgotten me. We tied the scraps of cloth to the thin, green branches of Kite's new tree, where they stayed for a year or so before the weather tore them away.

I didn't notice until after the ceremony was over that, in the distance, someone was flying a yellow kite in the thick, overcast sky. I suppose that's as good a way as any to make up a name for yourself. At my own naming ceremony, I asked to be called Paige, after a girl at my previous school. She wore purple butterfly clips in her hair, and had three Tamagotchis attached to the belt loops in her grey school trousers. I must have said it quiet, because I soon realised that Oak and Jara had misheard and were calling me Sage. By then, it was too late to correct them.

Jara had read somewhere that naming ceremonies helped adopted children to bond with their new families and keep the pain of their previous lives separate. Kite and I were fostered, not adopted, but Oak and Jara wanted us to pick new names anyway. The baby didn't need to choose its own name. It was being born into the life it would hold on to.

Oak and Jara took it in turns, a week at a time, to home-school Kite and me. The syllabus was loose, and moved around dramatically. Last week with Jara we'd learnt about Buddhism, using a cardboard box to create a life-sized cut-out of the Dalai Lama, which was now sagging in the corner of our bedroom. This week, Oak was teaching us about the medicinal properties of various wild plants, while Jara spent the afternoons upstairs meditating, or squeezing milk from her breasts into syringes in case the baby couldn't feed.

Oak instructed us to make a poster about natural remedies for warts. He gave us a book called *Wild Drugs* for research, which he'd bought from a friend who ran a campsite a few miles down the road. We sat on the floor of the study, surrounded by fragments of crayon, while Oak stood above us to work at his easel. Across nearby cities, Oak's paintings were hung in hippie shops and CBD cafés in the hope that they'd sell. His current piece was an entire solar system spiralled around the sun, although the sun was a golden lotus flower.

Sage? said Kite.

Yes.

How do you show the milk of a dandelion?

Just draw a droplet coming out the bottom of the stalk, I said.

For posters, Kite always drew, and I always wrote. I liked the monotonous, even task of letters, and found drawing frustrating. I could see the image in my mind, but my hands wouldn't always do what I wanted.

I was glad not to go to conventional school. At the school I went to when I lived with my mother, they'd made us climb ropes in a hall that had fluffy lumps of mashed potato in the corners, left over from lunch the day before. Once, the boy I had a crush on called me Big Mama in front of everyone.

I used to get up every morning and stand in the crack of doorway to my mother's bedroom. Some days, it would smell like ashtrays and old fruit. There might even have been a man in there, snoring under the covers. I'd go back to my bedroom, put my school uniform on and walk to school.

Other mornings, my mum would be alone, and it would smell slightly damp, but OK. I'd go over and touch her face. I don't want to go in today, I'd say.

She'd just frown in her sleep and roll over, which I'd take as a yes. I'd spend the day cutting paper chains and eating whole boxes of Coco Pops. Occasionally, my mother would wake up, and we'd go and try the 2p machines in the arcade, or sneak into a film in the cinema by pretending we'd only left the screen to go to the toilet. I saw lots of the second halves of films that way. Usually my mother didn't get up until evening. She'd go straight out, and wouldn't come back until five or six in the morning. I know because I'd sit up waiting, refusing to sleep until she was home.

It was all those absences that got us in trouble. The school sent a social worker around to the flat. I remember that day so clearly. I was wearing rabbit slippers and eating Skittles when I answered the door. The social worker said her name was June, like the month. I thought that was stupid. I told June that my mum was out, when really she was sleeping. I knew it wasn't normal, to sleep into the afternoon like that. When June came back the next day, I'd been to school just to prove a point. I was still in my uniform. This time, my mum really was out. June came in and poked around the flat a bit. When I got back from the toilet, I caught her looking in the fridge.

Isn't it time for your dinner soon? she said. Will your mum be back to cook for you?

I nodded, and hoped.

June stayed until past midnight. We watched *Bambi*, and then *Monsters, Inc.*, and then *Toy Story 2*. She kept trying to make me go to bed. Aren't you tired? she'd say. It's very late for little people like you.

I just kept shaking my head. I was convinced I could fight sleep longer than June. I wasn't that little. I knew that when my mother got back she'd be talking in her weird, syrupy voice, and using the walls to hold herself up. June would see there was something wrong. While I sat on the sofa and waited, I had this feeling that creatures were living between the layers of my skin, laying eggs and hatching a million times over. I kept scratching the insides of my elbows.

By the time my mother did get home I must have fallen asleep, because I woke to the sound of shouting. There was another social worker there too. June and my mother were in the kitchen. The other social worker asked me if there was anything special I wanted to take with me. It'll just be for a night or two, she said.

The last I remember of my mother is her face through the car window. Her skin had an orange glow from the street lights, and the rain on the glass threw dots of shadow across her cheeks.

We'd almost finished the poster when I heard the knock. It was crisp and cheerful, a little tune. I didn't realise until it happened that I'd been listening for it all day. Oak put his paintbrush down and went to answer the door. Jara, woken from her meditation, began to creak about upstairs. Kite kept colouring furiously, unconcerned by our visitor. Oak opened the front door, and I could hear Anthea's voice through the walls.

Kite had arrived at Oak and Jara's just as I had, in the middle of the night, carrying a plastic bag stuffed with clothes. Jara made him a bed on the floor of my bedroom from cushions and blankets. He didn't have pyjamas, and he stood by the black window in his underpants while he waited. He had a xylophone chest and skin so thin I could see the blue veins running down the side of his face. When Jara turned the light off and left, I watched his outline quivering in the bed.

Ben, I said. Don't be afraid. You can get in with me if you like.

He didn't say anything, but when I woke hours later, the winter sun slowly rising, I found his body tucked next to mine.

When I first moved to Oak and Jara's I suffered from night terrors, and I used to call out in my sleep. Oak stuffed a sock with dried lavender and put it under my pillow, and strung a wicker circle webbed with wool above my bed, to catch bad dreams before they got to me. I don't know if it was because of those things or not, but the night terrors faded, and eventually they went away completely. Before Kite's second night, I hid the lavender sock under his pillow and insisted that Oak move the dreamcatcher so it was hanging over Kite's bed instead. From then on, Kite slept fine.

Oak, Jara and Anthea appeared now in the doorway of the study. I could tell by their faces that the news was as I had expected: Kite was being taken away. Oak and

Jara had this stung, wet-eyed look that I knew came from trying not to cry in front of us.

As soon as Kite noticed Anthea, he became hysterical. His face got hot and streaky. I like it here, he begged. Please, please, I like it here.

Anthea explained how much his mother was looking forward to having him home. She's even painted your bedroom, Anthea said. And Ben? Your dad isn't going to be there.

Kite put his head in my lap. I could feel his wet face slipping against my bare shins. Anthea said that she'd be back for Kite in the morning. She gave me a small, sad nod as she left, and I scowled at her.

The front door clicked shut. Jara let out a faint wail. As I sat on the floor with Kite in my arms, I could feel the spiritual energy draining from my body. Let's go to the woods, I said.

I thought that things might feel better in our shelter. Oak and Jara were still by the front door, probably trying to work out the right words to say to us. Kite and I left the house through the back, hand in hand.

It was early evening by then, and the shadows were denser than before. Someone nearby was setting off fireworks even though it was still too light to see them. The noise cracked through the wood. I didn't know what to say, so I didn't say anything. We gathered up sticks to make a bonfire. We balanced them carefully against each other on the floor of the shelter, so that they stood upright. We didn't have matches to light the fire with, but we sat with our hands held out to it and pretended. I gave Kite a thin, pointed stick, and we toasted imaginary marshmallows, rotating them slowly like ducks in the window of a Chinese restaurant.

I pictured Kite in his newly painted bedroom, with the letters B-E-N nailed up above the bed. I thought about the kids at Kite's new school, bullying him for his uncut hair and doing sexy-girl MTV dance moves in the playground. I wondered who'd make Kite drink his apple cider vinegar, or give him arnica when he fell, or comb the lice out his hair. I wondered if, in a couple of years, he'd forget the order of poses in a sun salutation, or the myriad uses of coconut oil.

Kite's eyes were swollen from crying. He leant back against the log sofa and looked up at the inside of the tree. Maybe I'll just live here, he said.

I liked that idea. I'd sneak him sauerkraut sandwiches made from the falling-apart seedy loaves that Oak baked in the bread machine. I'd bring him Vet Barbie, a toothbrush, a few thick jumpers, a flask of hot oat milk. I'd tell Anthea that he'd run off in the night, and in a few weeks' time, once the baby was born and Anthea's visit was long forgotten, Kite could come back to the house and live with us incognito. Eventually, Oak and Jara could file for adoption papers for the two of us. We'd change our names legally and be siblings on paper.

Do you think it would really work, me staying here? Kite asked.

I considered the idea for a while. There would probably be a big search, I said. They wouldn't give up easily. You'd have to move from one shelter to another.

Kite shrugged. I could do that, he said.

Just then, the tree began to ring. Kite jumped. I'd forgotten about Oak and Jara's phone. I reached into the larder and answered. It was Oak.

Sage? The baby's coming. It's coming very fast.

Kite and I could hear Jara from the gate. Her calls were deep and long. When we got to her, the midwife still hadn't arrived. Labour had come on suddenly, and Oak had spent too long trying to find his phone before guessing that one of us had taken it. He'd had to leave Jara to borrow the neighbour's. If I'd had time to, I would have felt guilty.

Jara was knelt on all fours in the birthing pool. Her hair was stuck in long, tangled strands to her cheeks and neck, and in her huge pupils I could see my own face reflected. The pool was perfectly clear, lapping like a tiny sea. A small amount of light was coming from a weak eco-bulb in the corner, the full moon knocking at the window. When Oak poured a kettle of water into the pool, the steam came off in spirals. Kite and I took nubs of ice from a bowl on the floor and trailed them across Jara's face until they melted. The only sounds were her screams.

Jara had thought that she couldn't have children. The day she told Kite and me that she was pregnant, we made a cashew cheesecake to celebrate. Kite turned the blender on without attaching the lid properly and the mix splattered all over the kitchen. Oak licked a glob straight off the fridge door, and I licked some off the tap. Kite had it all over his face, in the ends of his hair. When I asked Jara why she was crying she said, I'm just so happy, Sage.

I knew, watching Jara in labour, that I never wanted to birth a baby of my own. It looked too much for me. Her whole body seemed to turn inside out. The baby's head came first, and then the rest of him slipped into the water. Jara reached down herself and pulled him up. She was shaking with exhaustion. The cord running between them was blue and twisty. I knew as soon as I saw the baby that there was something wrong. He was floppy and listless, with scrunched-up eyes. He reminded me of a dead rabbit I'd found in the garden once. Jara just held him, looking him over in disbelief. She didn't have the energy left to react. Oak rushed to her with a towel and began to rub the baby all over. Come on, he kept saying. Come on.

Kite and I just stood back, watching.

The baby's cry was the most beautiful sound I'd ever heard. It was sudden, and piercing. Hello, Oak said. Hello, there.

Oak slowed the rubbing, and stopped. I leant in next to him, behind Jara, to look. Up close, the baby smelt mulchy and sweet, like a mushroom just pulled from the ground. His skin flicked between colours and settled. His fish mouth breathed the steamy air. He opened his black, sparkly eyes to me and blinked.

Kite, I said. Look!

When Kite didn't come, I turned around to beckon him. It was then that I noticed he was gone. I padded out of the room without saying anything. I didn't want to disturb the baby. In the kitchen, the jar of almonds and dried apricots that Jara liked to snack on had been taken. The back door was slightly ajar, and the torch, which hung on a nail in the wall, was no longer there. I went out to the dark garden, up to the gate. The lights in the house just stretched to make the path visible. The flagstone felt cold against my bare feet. I stood at the gate and called for Kite. I called again and again. Out there, the navy woods looked endless.

Here Alone

The bar was called Opium. Emily walked straight from her office and entered through an unmarked black door held open with a brick. There was a slot of blue light humming out onto the pavement, and when she stepped into the corridor she noticed that a bare bulb dipped in blue plastic coating was hanging from the ceiling. The corridor led to flight of perforated metal stairs. Emily's heels kept getting caught in the holes on the way down.

There were more people than Emily had expected inside. The strange light shadowed their faces, brought out the imperfections in their skin. She ordered a whisky and stood by the seating area along the opposite wall. The sofas were leather and all taken. She took her phone out of her handbag and used it as a mirror to reapply her lipstick. The music got louder suddenly, or maybe it was just that a song came on that she recognised. She spent a moment trying to place it before giving up. A man came and stood near her. She cupped her glass in her hand like a bowl and swilled it slowly in circles. She knew that she wasn't a beautiful woman, but sexy felt like something not so far off.

You alright, she said.

The man looked at her. He was clean-shaven, with acne scars peppered across his cheeks, a large ridge in his forehead. His body was hard and triangular; his pale blue shirt a little tight around the shoulders, a little loose around the waist. Emily pursed her lips, looked into his eyes for too long a moment. This was her favourite part, the exchange of signs.

He stepped slightly closer. You want another? he said, and she raised her chin.

The drinks came. He told her he liked a woman who drank whisky. All the women I know drink white wine spritzers, he said. They order prosecco at dinner. It's juvenile.

She felt the whisky burn her oesophagus on its way down. She reached out and grazed her thumb along his jaw. There was enough drink in her to do that. He looked up in surprise. She felt her eyes get lazy for a second.

Come upstairs, she said. For a cigarette.

Emily brought her whisky with her, and when they got outside she knocked it back in one. She put the empty glass down on a plastic table dotted with raindrops. It had rained all day, but now the sky was cloudless, an expanse of perfect black behind the hazy dome of light pollution coming up off the city. Emily offered the man a cigarette. He held it between his lips while she lit it for him. Orange flared in his pupils.

I don't smoke usually, he said.

She shrugged. She didn't much care.

Are you here alone? he asked.

She nodded. He seemed to like that. He put his palm on the side of her arse and smoothed her back pocket while the bouncer looked on. She rolled onto the tips of her toes so that her face was close to his. She asked him a few questions about himself. When he spoke, she could taste his breath.

His name was Toby. He worked in a bank, though not with the money. He'd come to the bar with his girlfriend of two years, who'd ended their relationship and left without finishing her drink. He didn't ask Emily about her job. She told him she was a hairdresser, though she wasn't.

They caught the District Line. They made eye contact through their reflections in the windows, rather than looking straight at each other. She put her hand on his thigh, trailed her fingers up and down it, warming him up. She got closer and closer to touching his crotch, until he had to put his own hand on top of hers to stop her.

You're so hot, he whispered.

In her flat, she got two glasses from the kitchen and left him in her bedroom with the wine while she showered. She stood with her face lifted to the spray, the water coming off her dirty with make-up. She slicked her legs, armpits and crotch with a film of conditioner and shaved meticulously. Dark wires spun down the plughole. After, she reapplied her entire face, misting it with hairspray so it held.

In the bedroom, Toby had almost finished the wine. He looked bored, sitting on the edge of the bed with his legs crossed, scrolling his phone. You took your time, he said.

The sex was unremarkable. His hands were slippery, and it was only when he folded his arms behind his head that she began to enjoy herself. He made a sound when he came that was short and chirpy, a single high note on a piano. After, he pulled the covers over himself, suggesting he'd be staying the night.

How many people have you slept with? he said into the dark.

No one had ever asked her this before, though she'd hoped they would. Twenty, she replied.

A few years ago, on a bus, Emily had overheard one teenage girl explaining to another that the appropriate amount of people to have slept with is half your age plus seven. Emily's true number was in fact six, including Toby, and the spray can of deodorant she'd lost her virginity to at age fourteen. She hadn't come, but she hadn't minded. She knew even then that vaginal orgasms were for the most part a myth created by men. The can was slimy when it came out, with a speck of blood on the very tip. It reminded her of a tadpole, or the dots sometimes found on the yolk of an egg. She wiped it off with toilet paper and put it back in the cabinet over the bathroom sink. Her mother hated it when she borrowed her things.

You're the first woman I've gone to bed with in over a year, Toby said. He sounded proud of himself. Other than my girlfriend, he added. My ex-girlfriend, that is.

His hand sat on the mound of her pussy while he spoke, clammy and unmoving.

There were two weeks after when she didn't hear from Toby. She thought of him often. He'd got inside her like a tapeworm; she could feel him crawling around. She imagined her cheek pressed to Toby's neck on the night bus, his hand in hers on a bench by the river.

When he didn't reply to her third text, she began to consider the idea that he might not have existed at all. This was disproved when she found him on Facebook after searching through the night. Her relief was immense.

She put on a lot of bronzer and took a photograph of herself on her phone. She was topless, the frame of the camera cutting out just above her breasts. The time was three o'clock in the morning. She uploaded the photograph as her new profile picture and sent Toby a message.

This is Emily, from the other night. Have you been receiving my texts? I'd like to know in case there's a problem with my phone. Also, if you want to fuck me again, I'll consider it.

His reply flashed up on her phone three days later. She was at work. *Sorry, I've been distracted. Come to my friends' engagement party on Saturday.*

After that was a separate message with the address of the party, and another consisting of a single *x*.

Emily took herself out for a meal that evening to celebrate. She loved to eat alone. She chose an American-style diner and ordered pancakes with scrambled eggs and syrup. While waiting for her order, she rolled her shoulders and listened to the sinew crackle in her upper back, pressed her fingertips to the sticky tablecloth and pulled them away over and over. She cut each pancake into a grid and ate the squares one by one. She finished the eggs too, though they were cold by then, and mopped up the rest of the syrup with her index finger.

She walked home in the rain with her hood down, throwing her arms out in front of her. It was late by the time she reached her neighbourhood. Her feet throbbed.

She could smell syrup on her hands. She was waiting at a crossing when the realisation came to her. The fine rain was visible in the beams of car headlights, the moon hung low and bright like the inside of a freshly washed bowl. There were no stars, and when the cars stopped at the lights a cyclist continued to weave silent through the traffic. She was in love with Toby. This is what love felt like. Her hands came up over her face and she pressed them to her mouth. Laughter came at her suddenly, in waves, and made her upper body shudder and convulse. She laughed for so long that she missed the green man, and the traffic started up again with her still standing there. Toby, she said to herself, you cheeky bastard. She laughed so much that the muscles in her stomach started to hurt. She dashed out into the road without waiting for the traffic, and a man in a car had to slam on his brakes.

Stupid fucking bitch, he called out the crack in his window.

Emily wore white to the engagement party. The dress was silky and hugged her body in a way that looked haunting in dim lights. She used a lotion on her skin that was laced with tiny particles of glitter. It was a freezing night, but she didn't bring a coat.

The bride's mother opened the door and led Emily through to the living room. It was a big suburban house. Clear balloons filled with silver and white sequins bobbed in the corners. People stood in small groups drinking flutes of champagne with berries in them. Toby came over to her in quick strides, pulled her into the centre of the room, and used the knuckle of his index finger to lift her chin. He kissed her for a long time. Conversation hushed around them.

I can't believe he's got the nerve, one woman said. She spoke under her breath, but just loud enough. Another actually left the room; Emily felt their elbows brush as she passed.

Guys, this is Emily. Toby had both of his hands on her waist when he said this.

Congratulations, Emily said, to no one in particular.

Emily stood next to Toby all night. They spoke only to the men. The women huddled in the corners, looking at Emily and whispering. It got late. The older relatives left and the bride's parents went to bed. The guests were drunk by this point. Someone moved the coffee table to the corner of the room, turning the carpet into a makeshift dance floor. The couple getting married started dry-humping to a song by R. Kelly that Emily hadn't heard since she was a teenager. Toby pulled on her hand and she followed him to a large bathroom where a man was cutting lines of cocaine on the lid of the toilet. She had two.

Toby took her upstairs. They had sex in a bed that smelt of the fabric conditioner her mother always used.

They didn't make it up again after, leaving the sheet untucked at one corner and the duvet on the floor. On their way downstairs, Toby put his hand on her shoulder. She turned to face him. He was standing a few steps above her. His eyes kept shifting, beads of sweat hung around his temples.

If anyone asks, he said, tell them I'm your boyfriend.

Emily could feel the champagne fizzing in her stomach. I love you, she said.

Toby laughed a long, low chuckle. Perfect.

Downstairs, Toby left Emily in the living room to go and find his friend with the coke. She stayed in the corner with the balloons and moved her shoulders up and down in time to the music. Some of the women had formed a ring around the bride, who was spinning in small, unsteady circles. After a few minutes, the ring broke open, and one of the women stepped out. She came and stood next to Emily, her arms crossed over her chest. She had blonde hair gathered in a neat knot at the base of her neck, a few feathery strands left loose around her face. Her nails were French manicured.

I think it's time I introduced myself, she said. I'm Mia. The ex.

Emily extended her hand. Mia didn't reach for it. On the dance floor, the bride fell down onto the carpet. The other women shrieked and crowded around her. Babe, one of them shouted. Babe, Babe.

The bride appeared to be out cold. Emily looked back at Mia, who didn't seem to have noticed.

We only broke up a few weeks ago, said Mia. We didn't even break up, actually. *Space* was the word I used.

Emily reached for a half-drunk glass of champagne on the mantelpiece. Is this yours? she said.

Mia shook her head. It's pretty weird that he brought you here, to be honest. We've known all these people since school.

I don't think it's that weird.

Don't you see what he's doing? He's been calling me every day. He's trying to make me jealous. He isn't actually interested in you.

Emily raised her eyebrows, craned her neck a little backwards. He just wanted to introduce his new girlfriend to his friends, she said.

On the dance floor, someone threw a glass of water over the bride. She stirred and pushed herself up onto her elbows. People exchanged glances, relieved. The bride surveyed the room, unsure where she was.

Girlfriend? said Mia.

Emily nodded, sipped the champagne.

The bride came to. She brought her fingers to her cheek and touched the skin there, which was still wet. You've ruined my make-up, she screamed. Black tears cut through her foundation, and she beat her fists against the carpet. Where's Aaron? Where *is* Aaron? He can't fucking see me like this.

Emily looked for Toby all through the house. She wanted to leave. The coke had worn off and given her a headache. When she couldn't find him, she got her phone and called six times. Mia, too, was nowhere to be seen.

In the kitchen, Emily helped herself to a bottle of champagne from the ice bucket on the counter. She drank the first glass quickly and poured another. Soon the whole bottle was gone. Ravenous, she finished the plate of cold cuts that had been laid out all evening. They'd hardened slightly at the edges, but were otherwise good.

She went to check the garden. Toby wasn't there, only the groom and another man sitting side by side on the edge of the patio, taking hits from a bong. She asked them if they'd seen Toby, and they looked at each other and shrugged.

Can I have some? she said.

Emily wasn't a big smoker. The groom spent a long time talking her through the process. Did it work? he asked, after.

She looked out into the night. I don't know, she said.

Here, have another.

She sucked the smoke diligently this time, pulling it back into her lungs. There you go, said the groom.

Emily felt pleased with herself, and quickly very nauseous. She lay down on the grass. The groom and his friend giggled. Emily rolled onto her side. A burp rose in her throat, the tang of meat. She knew it was only a matter of time before she threw up. She took her phone from her purse, held it close to her face, and sent Toby a text.

were u serious when u asked me to be ur gf?

Emily woke at sunrise. The grass was grey with frost and crunched beneath her weight. Someone had thrown a sleeping bag over her, now wet with dew. She went to check the time on her phone, and found that the battery had died. Through the windows, she could see that the lights in the house were turned off, the curtains of the bedrooms drawn. She stood up, straightened her dress, and combed her hair with her fingers. There were clumps of something gummy, slightly frozen, and when she brought her hand to her nose she understood that it was vomit. Emily folded the sleeping bag, sat it on the mat by the back door, and let herself out through the side gate.

She plugged her phone in to charge the moment she got back to her flat, sitting on the floor by the socket until the screen lit up. There was no returned call from Toby, no reply to her text. She waited on him for days, calling in sick to work three times in a row. Life passed slowly, slots of time held together by checking her phone. She refreshed Toby's Facebook profile over and over, but he didn't make a single post. She could tell he was alive only by the small green circle next to his name in the Messenger app.

On Friday, six days since she'd last seen Toby and three weeks since she'd first met him, Emily walked from her office to Opium. The blue light on the pavement hummed just the same. She sat up at the bar, her stool angled towards the stairway, drinking gin and tonics back to back. The night was busy. Every time a customer descended the metal stairs Emily checked to see if they were Toby.

She got to a point where she didn't need to order from the bartender in words, but simply with a gesture to her empty glass. When he asked her to leave, he was polite about it. Last orders had been and gone, and she was the last customer inside. The bartender spoke slowly, too aware of how much Emily had drunk.

She picked the lime wedge out of her glass and began to eat it, looking right at him as she did so. D'you think I'm attractive? she said.

He picked up her glass and turned it upside down over the sink. Sure. If you like.

Emily paid for her drinks with a tap of her debit card, got up from her stool and made her way slowly up the stairs. In the taxi home, she called Toby eighteen times.

That night, Emily slept fully clothed, not even removing her shoes. She woke to her ringtone. It was nine o'clock in the morning. She reached for her phone, and found that the name on the screen was Toby's. Her hangover evaporated, and she felt filled instead with something like helium; there was a sensation of floating upwards from her body.

Hello, she said.

The phone made a swishing noise, a tap.

Hello, she said again.

The phone went quiet. Emily's ear canal pulsed in anticipation of Toby's voice — the halting, sarcastic way in which he spoke — but instead the phone made a series of small ticks, after which the swishing started up again, this time a pace faster. It was a pocket call. Toby had stopped at some lights, perhaps, and now was crossing the road. Emily sank back into her body, winded.

The morning after the engagement party, she'd got lost on her way to the train station. She'd thought she could remember the route, having made it the night before, but now each suburban street looked the same. Her phone was dead, the windscreens of the parked cars were iced over. She ached all through her body. The smell of vomit wafted from her hair into her mouth with each step. She considered giving up many times — stopping to sleep on the frosted earth beneath the hedges that lined the front gardens — but each time, she'd thought of

Toby, and the text that was waiting in her phone: *Are you kidding? Of course I was serious.*

Now, Emily sat upright in bed and removed her phone from her ear so the sounds of Toby's walking became faint. She reread his name on the screen, cracked the bones in her neck and tapped the red call button to hang up. In a few more taps, she'd blocked Toby's number. It was as sudden as that, and once it was done, a calmness came over her. She lay back, her limbs spread wide across the mattress.

Emily slept for two and a half hours. When she woke, she was hungry. She removed yesterday's clothes and shoes, showered and dressed, then walked four blocks from her flat to an Italian restaurant. She'd passed it many times, but had never been inside. It had red-and-white checked tablecloths, an unlit, semi-melted candlestick on each table, a thick layer of dust along the windowpanes. The menu was translated into four languages, each version pinned to the fake brick wall that lined the interior. The restaurant had no other customers. Emily sat at a table in the far corner and ordered a carbonara. It came in no time, the waiter shuffling out from nowhere and leaving again just as briskly. Emily pinched the end of a strand of spaghetti between her thumb and forefinger, lifted it from the plate, then lowered it into her open mouth. When the strand was around halfway in, she closed her lips around it and sucked. The yolky sauce dripped down her chin, a piece of bacon fell back to her plate. She repeated the process with another strand of spaghetti, and another. Her fork sat untouched on the paper napkin.

The Mothers and the Girls

The girls woke, for the third day in a row, to rain. The tent smelt like pond. They passed items of clothing back and forth, pressing their faces into them.

Wet, or cold?

Wet.

These?

Cold, I think.

The girls' mothers were asleep in the next tent over. The girls unzipped the nylon door and crouched. The mothers were using their coats as pillows. There was an empty beer can in there, filled with cigarette ends.

It's Monday, said one girl.

You need to call our schools, said the other. You need to tell them we're sick.

Mm-hm, said the mothers.

It was late June, the start of the festival season, and school hadn't broken up yet. The girls were thirteen. One had a stomach bug, the other had tonsillitis.

There was a caravan in the corner of the field where the girls' tent was pitched. Inside the caravan was warm and dry. The bed had a real mattress, a real duvet. Lisa, who owned the caravan, sat in a camping chair under a tarp shelter, drinking grainy tea and barking at visitors to take their wellies off.

Is there room inside? asked the girls.

Don't think so, loves. The littlies beat you to it.

As always, the younger kids got priority. They sat in there all day, eating boiled hotdogs and watching downloaded Pixar films on a brick laptop, the colours squirming in their wet eyes.

The girls spent the morning roaming the site, taking turns to push each other around in a wheelbarrow. For lunch they picked up free daal from the Hare Krishnas and sat on burlap sacks to eat, right in the middle of the spiegeltent, while volunteers in hi-vis stepped over them, carrying huge steel poles and rounds of rope.

In the afternoon, the girls approached a few stalls in the process of being built, and asked to swap an hour's work with the traders for treats. They painted a sign. They transported the wheelbarrow, filled with bags of ice, from one end of site to another. In return, they received polystyrene cups of hot chocolate and one pair of glittery leggings.

The mud was liquid from the rain, and when night came the floodlights made it glisten. The girls stole cups of flat cider from a keg that the adults kept hidden under the caravan. They drank it in the tent with their legs interwoven, telling each other outlandish stories about their lives back home while the LED torch cast their faces pale green.

Three boys from school bet money on who could kiss me first.

Real money?

Seven pounds.

Who won?

Jasper. He's the best-looking. His sister's famous. She was on *The X Factor* last year. She came second. Did you watch?

No.

The film crew went to Jasper's house to interview his parents. Jasper was in it, saying how much his sister deserved to win. He looked so hot in the clip. My whole year went crazy. He's been recognised on the street.

Did she deserve to win?

Definitely. She was the best on it. The only reason she didn't is because the other guy had cerebral palsy.

My dad's been on TV loads.

How come?

He was a child actor. You can still find the adverts on YouTube. There's one where he bites the ends off a Penguin bar and drinks milk through it. He got paid in Penguins, a whole lifetime supply.

He must have eaten them all by now.

They send him a big crate whenever he runs out. He doesn't have a fixed address at the moment, but once he does they'll start it up again. He says he's sick of Penguins anyway.

He can give them to me.

That's what I said!

Is that why he's a junkie then, like Macaulay Culkin?

My dad's not a junkie.

Course he is. My mum told me.

She must be thinking of someone else. He's getting me an iPhone. I've said I want one of those cases with liquid trapped in it like a lava lamp, and little plastic fish that move around.

Oh yeah, I've seen those. This girl I know had one. Hilary. She always used to chew it in lessons, and then one day it leaked in her mouth and she had to go to hospital to have her stomach pumped. Her whole tongue's bright blue, like she's eaten a Toxic Waste, and they say it'll never go away.

The girls' mothers were trapeze artists. They had an act together, touring various festivals over the summer. The mothers had been performing for the girls' entire lives, and the girls had attended every single show. As babies, they were parked up at the edge of the stage in their buggies. As children, they joined the audience, pushing their way to the front. Now the girls always sat in the centre of the marquee floor to watch, their necks flung back, barely taking a breath as their mothers hung above them, perfectly synchronised, the muscles tight under their skin.

Every year, the show remained popular. The mothers knew many faces in the festival circuit who always made the effort to come. Punters would drop in by accident, looking for a bar or something to eat, and find themselves mesmerised.

The girls never felt prouder of their mothers than when watching them perform. No two women were so beautiful, so able to take flight. At home, the mothers spent the winters smoking cigarettes in the bathtub and making sandwiches for dinner. The girls wouldn't see each other for months at a time. One lived in Edinburgh, the other in Bristol. But the summers were spent together, as a four, driving from one site to another: the mothers up front, singing in harmony with the radio, the girls in the back, padded with sleeping bags, fishing tangerines from a net.

It was Wednesday when the rain finally stopped. The sky ran blue. Everyone was excited, hanging their wet bedding out to dry. Lisa sliced up a watermelon and handed out chunks to the little kids. The festival wouldn't officially start until the evening of the following day, but already the site had started to fill with more and more people. The mud turned sticky from the sun and started to smell sulphurous. Walking took effort, pushing the wheelbarrow was near impossible. The girls abandoned it in a bush and went to check if anything new had popped up in the Craft Field. This was where the girls met River.

It was River's dad they spoke to first. He was a carpenter, running a workshop on woodwork. The girls went over to ask if they could help set up in exchange for a free lesson over the weekend. They wanted to make bows and arrows.

You're fine, girls, he said. There's not much that needs doing. Come by once we're up and running, though. We'll see if we can sort you out.

Just as the girls were turning away, River climbed out the back of a van. He was carrying a plastic tub filled with sawdust. His hair was completely shaved other than a single, matted strand that hung down the back of his neck, and his earlobes were puckered and gummy from using stretchers.

You alright? said River.

The girls nodded.

River picked a diabolo up from the floor, and started doing tricks. There was mud on the sticks and on his hands. The girls lifted their heads up and down in unison, watching the diabolo like dogs. River pedalled the sticks, faster and faster, before flinging the diabolo hard into the sky. The sun glinted electric off the metal and hurt the girls' eyes. River held the string taut, and when the diabolo came down, humming, he caught it with what seemed to be no effort at all. The girls were entranced. River held a conversation while he did this.

You two sisters?

The girls exchanged looks. Yes, said one.

Twins, said the other.

How old are you?

Fifteen, you?

Sixteen, said River.

When d'you arrive?

Just this morning. Drove from Cornwall.

You from there?

Yeah. What about you two?

Bris——, said one.

Edinburgh, said the other.

You don't sound Scottish.

We're not.

You always talk at the same time?

No.

You wanna show me around?

Sure.

River got back into the van, and came out again with three muesli bars. He gave one to each of the girls. They ate as they walked, River in the middle, the girls either side looking up at him. He smelt like a rabbit hutch.

The girls showed River all they could think to show. There was the sculpture of the gecko made of old CDs. There was VIP Camping, its lines of bell tents strung with bunting, and green coconuts given out to celebrities on arrival. There was the main stage, where you could hear your own voice bounce back when you shouted. There was the Kids' Field, with the spinning teacups that weren't working yet but that you could sit in when it rained. There was the viewing tower with the spiral staircase, and underneath there was the portaloo cubicle where the girls had written their names in permanent marker on the inside of the door. They gave River the pen to add his own name, and instead he drew a long river, meandering all the way down, cutting between the girls' names.

Cool, said the girls. Their own names didn't have symbols that they could think of.

They invited River back to their campsite. The sun was low by then. The girls needed more layers on, and they were hungry. Their mothers were there, sitting on an old sofa with a ripped cover, passing a bottle of red wine between them. They were both wearing dirty fur coats, but their silver eyeliner was impeccable.

Where'd you get that? said the girls, meaning the sofa.

Chris arrived today, said one mother. He bought it.

The girls didn't know who Chris was. Oh, they said. Who's this?

River.

River nodded at the mothers.

You alright, precious? one said.

Yeah, said River.

The girls went to their tent and found some fleeces to put on under their jackets. From inside, they could hear their mothers talking to River. They asked him who his dad was. The mothers liked to act as if they knew every-one on site, which the girls found irritating.

Graham, you said?

Yeah. Runs a woodwork stall.

Craft Field?

Yeah.

Mm. Don't know him, do we?

Not sure.

He single?

Um.

Sorry, love. Embarrassing you!

The mothers' laughter rang like a wind chime. In the tent, the girls found a multipack of crisps. They brought a bag out for River.

Good flirting, said the mother of the girl who passed River the crisps.

The girls turned to go. River followed and stepped between them, falling into pace.

I thought you guys said you were twins, said River.

We didn't say that.

River looked from one girl to the other. Whatever, he said. Your mums are cool.

Yeah, said the girls. We know.

The edge of the site sloped upwards and from the top of the hill you could see over the tall, grey fence. Countryside stretched out like patchwork, split by lines of trees. The sky had started to orange. They sat down in a row on the grass. River took some cupcakes from his pocket that were wrapped in greaseproof paper.

They're space cakes, he said.

The girls looked at the icing. It was purple and blue, swirled together with a toothpick. They assumed the name had something to do with the decoration. The cakes tasted earthy, but good.

We didn't take you for a baker, the girls said.

Means to an end, River said. His mouth was full of cake.

The girls weren't sure what he meant, but they laughed.

It took half an hour or so for things to turn strange. The girls started to notice their conversations going around in circles, always coming back to the same point. It was cosmic; everything seemed linked to everything else.

It's all connected, the girls said.

They were lying on their backs now, the grass cold through their jackets, each holding one of River's hands. The sky was black, sprinkled with crystals of salt. The moon made polite conversation. The trees stood up and waved.

The girls weren't sure who started it, the giggling. Perhaps it was River. Perhaps it was Moon. The laughter swelled in their bellies, made their whole bodies seize, and then broke out finally in a long, steady stream. It lasted for what felt like hours. It seemed that it would never end. They didn't mind. It felt good. They were inflated as balloons, full with wonder.

At some point, they stood up.

What time is it? said River. He seemed to have been dozing.

There is no time, said the girls.

On the walk to the tent, one of the girls pointed to the ground. There was a huge puzzle piece sitting on top of the mud. It was holographic. In it, River's face shimmered and flipped like a stingray.

Look, said one girl.

Wow, said the other.

The girls bent down to pick it up. In their hands, the puzzle piece became not a puzzle piece at all, but a paper plate of stir-fried noodles. The plate dropped, and the noodles hung from their fingers, claggy and tangled. The girls looked at their hands, amused.

Are you two alright? said River.

The girls flashed him their black eyes. We'd forgotten you were there, they said. They took his hands again in their own, greased now with oil and soy sauce, and walked on.

At the campsite, the mothers were pouring rum into bottles of ginger beer. Some of their friends were milling around, smoking. There was music playing from a portable speaker.

We're off out, said the mothers to the girls.

The girls giggled.

Are you two high? said the mothers.

No, said the girls.

The mothers looked at each other and laughed. River, said one. We knew you'd be trouble.

River shrugged. Sorry, he said.

The tent was small for the three of them. River took his shirt off, and the girls stayed dressed. They moved their hands over his chest while he talked. He told them stories he'd heard on the news, like of a parrot who used his owner's Alexa to order his favourite foods.

He likes watermelon, said River. And broccoli.

Next, he told them about two robots who, when introduced as part of a study, invented their own language and had a conversation that humans still can't unpick, potentially about world domination.

The girls listened and didn't respond. The stories seemed to come from another planet entirely. The girls were tired, their eyes drooping, when the paranoia came.

Go to sleep, go to sleep, the girls said, inside their heads.

They lay still, listening to each other breathing. They were convinced they were going to die. Either they would kill each other, or River would kill them. There was no telling which way it would go. River's chest hair sprung underneath their clammy palms. His body twitched with a sleep they were convinced he was faking. The darkness was full of shapes.

In the morning, to their surprise, the girls woke alive. River, too, was breathing the stale tent air. There weren't even any bruises; the girls checked. The sun came through the opening in the nylon door and made a rainbow. Outside, the little kids were asking for baked beans.

The girls lifted their heads from the cushions of River's upper arms and looked at each other.

Did you feel how I felt?

I think it was the cake.

I wonder if he has more.

One of the girls leant forward and brushed her lips, very softly, against River's cheek. On the opposite side, the other girl did the same. River opened his eyes a crack and smiled.

You two are sweet, he said.

The girls got up and went outside. Their skin was damp from the hot tent, and their clothes were sticking to their bodies. Lisa was sitting outside her caravan, warming coffee on the ashes of a burnt-out fire. A few of the little kids had put wellies on over their pyjama bottoms and were wandering around, looking for money or lighters that people had dropped on their way to bed. The girls brushed their teeth with one toothbrush. River wandered over to the little kids, started throwing them in the air and catching them.

Under the caravan, one of the mothers was asleep. Her head stuck out of the caravan's shadow. Her hand looked bright against the grass. Her cheeks were flecked with glitter and mascara. One of the girls pulled a bottle of water from the tent and left it by her mother's head for when she woke up. After, the girl unzipped her mother's bumbag and pulled out a twenty-pound note. A small plastic baggie came with it, sailed to the ground like a feather.

Let's get breakfast, the girl said.

The girls and River bought fried egg baps and banana milkshakes from a gazebo by the main stage. Lots of the stalls weren't properly set up yet, so this one had queues out the door. River still hadn't put his T-shirt back on from the night before. His skin was lighter on his chest and shoulders than on his forearms. He spilt ketchup on his left nipple, and used his finger to slick it off.

One of the girls squeezed his cheek, as if he were a little boy. The other put her palm on his bare shoulder and stroked.

They went up the Craft Field, the girls walking on either side of River. River's dad was putting the finishing touches to his stall. He asked for River's help whittling a few examples of things that the workshop would offer.

River got started on a spoon. The girls sat and watched.

How do you get it so smooth? they asked.

What sort of wood is that?

Have you ever cut yourself?

Don't you get afraid?

River's dad looked on, chuckling. After a while, he got up and handed the girls two blocks of light wood and two knives.

Face the blades away from yourselves now, he said.

The girls went quiet while they were working, pausing only occasionally to look up at River, who was paying them no attention at all. The only sounds were of the wood taking shape, flecks collecting in the folds of their knees. They'd been whittling for around half an hour when one of the girls let out a high-pitched cry.

I've cut myself, said the girl. She held up her thumb, and squeezed. The cut wasn't deep, but she did manage to draw a few drops of blood.

Look River, she said. It hurts.

River went to the van and came out with a green plastic box. Inside were plasters, and he wrapped one around the cut. The girl started to weep, and he took her face in his hands. His thumbnails were thick lines of dirt.

It's OK, he said. Listen, it's OK.

The girl looked at her reflection in his eyes. She blinked heavily and a few more tears spilt. He kissed her on the forehead.

It's OK, he said again.

The girl nodded, sniffing. River let go of her face and went back to his work. The other girl, the one who hadn't been cut, reached out and put her carving on River's knee.

I'm finished, she said.

The block of wood, oblong before, was now a small bird. It had a long, thin beak and wings chiselled with such care that they appeared almost feathered. River picked the bird up gingerly and held it to the sunlight. In his fingers, it soared.

That's unbelievable, he said. I could never carve anything like that. Have you done this before?

The girl shook her head. Never, she said.

The other girl hadn't made much headway. Her carving looked like an aubergine. She rolled the wood away as if she'd had nothing to do with it.

River got up to show the bird to his dad. Look at this, he called, as he was walking away.

You made that cut on purpose, one girl whispered to the other.

The girl with the plaster let out a quiet laugh. I can't believe you said you've never whittled before.

The girls didn't say anything after that. It was clear that neither had lost, and yet neither had won. They just looked each other over, narrowed eyes scanning, until River came back and sat between them.

Did your dad like the bird? said one girl.

My thumb's starting to throb, said the other.

The mothers' trapeze performance was that evening. The girls stole a bottle of dark rum from the boot of the car attached to Lisa's caravan. They drank it straight, sitting on the dirty tarpaulin floor of the Circus Stage, sharing with River, in hot little sips that made the girls shudder. By the time the mothers appeared above them, the world had become soft.

The mothers had stuck tiny gems to the centres of their eyelids that glinted at certain angles. Throughout the performance, the girls took turns to smile at River, or touch him lightly on the leg. They continued to drink the rum, uncrossing their ankles intermittently to shake the pins and needles from their feet. For their last act, the mothers swung their trapezes like pendulums across the tent, peddling back and forth with their bodies before letting the bars slip, in perfect unison, from their hands. The audience became eerily quiet as the mothers flew through the nothing air like used tissues in their white silk dresses, arms thrown out as wings might be. Their bodies traced a perfect X against the ceiling of the tent. At the very last moment, they caught hold of the opposite bar and found safety. The crowd gasped. The girls turned and looked at River. He appeared breathless, slightly giddy.

Incredible, he said. Just magic.

The girls raised their eyebrows. We too have tricks up our sleeves, they said.

The mothers, panting, left their trapezes secured at the platform at the top of the ladder before climbing down and disappearing backstage. The girls split the last of the rum. Between them, River cheered.

That night, the festival well and truly began. There were tents with music, and lights of all colours. The girls held hands and danced around River in a ring. Whenever he spoke, the girls could only see his mouth moving. The three of them walked from one stage to another every hour or so, crossing the dried mud like antelope to a watering hole, uneven on their wonky legs. Strangers in crowds gave them swigs of drinks mixed in plastic bottles: Skittles vodka, flat Aperol spritz. Between stages, the girls found a cardboard crate of Strongbow around the back of the portaloos, and River filled his backpack with dented cans.

It was just starting to get light when one of the girls noticed that the other was kissing River. They were at the main stage. The music sounded dense; there was something wrong with the acoustics. The silhouette of River's face meeting the girl's flashed purple, then fuchsia. The girl who was kissing River was the same girl who had carved the aubergine. When they stopped kissing, she looked over to the other girl, who had pretended not to notice and was dancing. River took the arm of the girl he hadn't kissed and started to twirl her around. The girl who had kissed River stood watching the girl who hadn't. Their eyes met. It only lasted a second, but both were struck by the sadness in the other's face.

At around five o'clock in the morning, River suggested climbing the viewing tower. The sun was just rising, and the girl who'd kissed River was now holding his hand. When they got to the foot of the tower, the girl who hadn't stopped.

I'm tired, she called ahead. I think I'm going to go to bed.

River turned around. Come up with us, he said. The light's beautiful.

The girl who hadn't shook her head. You two go, she said.

River started to climb the spiral staircase of the viewing tower. The girl who had went with him, and the girl who hadn't stayed behind. She was standing a few steps from a fire pit, where a white man with dreadlocks to his waist was reciting a poem to a couple who'd fallen asleep. She watched River and the girl who had as they climbed. Their silhouettes were black against the new sun, holding hands like a paper-doll chain. The girl who hadn't sighed, then followed.

The stairs looped around a huge steel pole. It was impossible not to think about how the whole structure had been put together a week before, and would be taken down the following week. From the top, the sky was yellow, the hills in the distance the sharp, neon green of highlighter pens. On the ground, the dried mud glittered with strewn bottle caps. The music from all the different venues mashed into a constant, gentle hum, and birds could be heard whistling from the trees.

You came, said River.

The girl who had kissed River stood on his left, and the girl who hadn't stood on his right. He put his arms around their shoulders. His chest rose slowly between them, and fell. The girl who had reached up to kiss him again, and he smiled and turned his mouth to her. They kissed for a long time. The girl who hadn't could hear the sounds of it, soft and wet as eating. River's hand was still on her shoulder.

After, River turned to the girl who hadn't and pressed his lips to hers. She held her face still, the breath from his nose tickling her upper lip. He pushed his tongue inside her mouth very gently, and she let him.

What are you doing? said the girl who had.

The girl who hadn't, who was now also the girl who had, pulled away from River. Stop, she said.

River turned so that his back was against the metal railing, and raised his palms upwards. Sorry, he said. I thought that's what this was.

The girls looked at each other.

I thought you liked me, one girl said.

I thought you changed your mind, said the other.

River frowned at the view. The sun shone through the railings. Just then, the viewpoint became crowded. The girls had been concentrating on River so hard that they hadn't heard anyone coming up the stairs. There were seven or eight people. The girls and River had to press their bodies up to the railings to make room. The girls vaguely recognised some of the faces, and when the crowd parted, their mothers were standing in the middle of it. The mothers were holding tin cups of chai. A man was unscrewing the cap of his hip flask in order to pour its contents into the cups.

Look who it is, said the mothers.

Everyone looked. Another of the friends was collecting white powder in the growth of his fingernail. When he realised who the girls were, he stopped and put the baggie away.

You three been having fun? said the mothers.

Yes, said the girls.

Did you see the headliner tonight? said one of their friends.

The girls looked at each other, unsure.

The mothers laughed, and their friends joined in. You missed the show of a lifetime, the mothers said.

Maybe of your lifetime, said one of the girls.

Anyway, said the other. We were just on our way to bed.

The mothers grinned. Why?

The girls gestured towards the view. It's daylight, said one.

The birds are singing, said the other.

Another of the friends, who was wearing cat ears and cowboy boots, snickered. Are you sure they're yours? he said.

Everyone laughed again. When the girls made to leave, the group stepped aside to let them. Night girls, sang the mothers. Night River.

Night, said River.

The girls didn't reply.

River had one last can of Strongbow in his backpack, and the three of them shared it as they walked to the campsite. It was warm, but they drank it anyway. The music in most places had finished, and the girls didn't speak to fill the silence.

As they passed the Circus Stage, one of the girls stopped and unzipped the canvas door. There were no lights on in there, other than a single bulb dangling from the centre of the ceiling. The steps of the ladder glinted, the trapezes cast shadows across the packed dirt floor. Let's go inside, said the girl. I have an idea.

She took the other girl's hand and they stepped together inside the tent.

River hung back. We're not supposed to go in there, are we?

The girls laughed. We do what we want, they said.

They started to climb the rungs of the ladder. First one, then the other.

What are you doing? called River. He stepped further inside the tent.

We want to show you a trick, said the girls.

No, said River. Don't.

The girls climbed back down the ladder again. When their feet touched the floor, River's relief was audible.

I know a way you can stop us, one of the girls said.

Choose, said the other.

River shook his head. What do you mean?

You know what we mean, said one girl.

Choose between us, said the other.

Don't make me do that, said River.

The girls giggled. They shoved River. It was supposed to be a jokey shove, but he staggered backwards. Stop being silly, they said. Just choose.

River bit his lip. I choose both, he said.

The girls frowned. You're talking nonsense. Choose.

I choose neither, said River.

The girls shrugged. Suit yourself, they said. They walked back over to the ladder again.

Please, said River. The safety net's been put away. You could hurt yourselves.

The girls laughed. What do you care, they said.

The girls climbed the ladder unhurriedly, rung by rung. At the top, they pulled themselves onto the platform. The air felt cooler up there. When the girls looked down, their stomachs flipped.

Come down, said River. I'm begging you.

The girls took the twin trapezes from the nail where they hung. Their laughter rose and filled the tent.

Please, called River, his voice wavering. That's enough.

The girls' faces looked waxen and rounded in the dim light, like cherubs in an oil painting. We have one final trick, they said, and then they jumped.

Blue 4eva

Stella's lying on a sun lounger, and then her book is wet. She watches the dots darken the paper as they sink in. On the surface of the pool, tiny blue waves ricochet out, the sun skittering off them. Underneath is the dark silhouette of a girl. She swims the whole length without coming up for air. When she breaks the surface, she puts her arms on the tiled edge and rests her chin in the crook of her wrists. Stella looks back at her book.

Hey, you. I see you.

The girl is Blue, a friend of Jasmine's from school. Her eyes are narrowed to the sun. Under her armpit, Stella notices a tangle of dark hair, slicked down like a clump pulled from the plughole.

You the baby, then?

Guess so.

Blue pushes off into the water again, floating on her back with her head lifted. Stella can't think of anything good to say, and eventually Blue lets her ears slip under. The cicadas sing in the background like a phone vibrating.

Stella's mother married Jasmine's father in February. Stella is twelve, Jasmine is eighteen. For their honeymoon, Claire and Frank went to Costa Rica. Stella and Jasmine weren't invited. When they returned home, Frank announced that he'd booked three weeks in a villa on the smallest island in the Balearics, to make up for it. Jasmine was over from her mother's. Claire had baked a lemon drizzle.

Cake's for children, said Jasmine. And I'm not coming.

They've been on holiday for five days. No one asked what it was that made Jasmine change her mind and join them. Stella suspects she's only here to ensure that everyone has as difficult a time as possible. Jasmine knocks hard on the bathroom door whenever Stella's in the shower. She steals Stella's sun lounger the moment she gets in the pool.

This is my spot, Jasmine says when Stella comes back, waving to the strip of shade where the other lounger waits.

There are other things too, little things that Stella can't prove. She woke up one morning itchy with bites, and discovered a tiny hole in her mosquito net that she was sure hadn't been there when she'd fallen asleep. Another time, someone moved her book into the sun and left it for hours, so the glue in the spine melted and the pages started falling out.

Back in England, Stella's bedroom used to be Jasmine's. Everything in it is either white or beige. There's a low bed, a rug made of woven straw, and a pale, angular desk beneath a desktop computer, the monitor the size of a plasma television. Stella had never had her own computer before.

I don't know if that's a good idea, Claire said, when she saw.

Frank only winked at Stella. She's in secondary now. She might need it for homework.

It was the day they'd moved in. Frank had already ordered pizzas for dinner, then opened up the shed in the garden to reveal an expensive-looking bike, bright green with yellow lightning bolts across the handlebars. If this was what having a dad was, Stella could get used to it.

In fact, Stella's school made a point not to set homework on the computer. When Stella found out about the holiday, it was the first time she used the desktop for anything other than video games. She looked up the island and sat for hours, hovering her mouse over the images. She didn't go downstairs again all evening, and Jasmine left without saying goodbye. The water looked so clear Stella could see the shadows of the boats on the sand at the bottom of the sea. She thought that when she swam in it, she'd be able to watch the fish drifting beneath her, an aquarium without the glass.

Out here, Stella spends most of her time with Frank and Claire, while Jasmine stays alone in the villa. In the mornings, they set up on the beach and eat peaches in the shade of a parasol. Stella climbs onto Frank's shoulders and dives off them into the sea. In the afternoons, they wander the dusty towns, stopping in cafés and stone churches to drink coffee or light candles, Frank's camera swinging around his neck. Frank buys Stella little gifts wherever they go: a key ring with a lizard on it, a pair of canvas espadrilles. Sometimes he puts his hand on Claire's waist while they're walking, and pulls her into him. Claire looks at Stella sideways, a little embarrassed.

In the evenings, back at the villa, the three of them sit on the veranda. Frank cuts slivers of manchego with a satisfying contraption while Claire mixes sangria in a big glass jug. Last night, for the first time, Jasmine came outside and poured herself a glass.

OK kids, she said. Fun's over. You can all stop pretending to be functional now.

Frank cut a slice of manchego and laid it down in front of her. Jasmine didn't touch her cheese. After some minutes, she announced that she'd invited Blue out to join them.

Frank threaded his fingers together on the table. The point of this trip, he said, was to spend time together as a four.

Right. And how is that working out for you?

Frank went quiet after that, and Blue wasn't mentioned again all evening. By morning, Stella had forgotten about her. By afternoon, here she was.

Blue lifts herself out of the pool and sits on the edge, leaning back on her long arms to feel the sun on her chest. She spreads her legs like a man, not seeming to worry that the flesh of her thighs looks bigger pressed against the tiles. Fuck me, it's hot.

Stella loves it when people swear in front of her. Tell me about it, she says.

A sound comes from behind the dry stone wall that separates the villa from the farmland around it. The sound is like a tiny sneeze, or the extending of a plastic straw. Stella's used to these sounds by now, but Blue whips her head over her shoulder to look.

No. Sorry, no. As you were.

Blue turns her head back to its previous position. Frank appears from behind the wall. Damn, he says. Lost it.

Blue laughs. Am I going to feature in an upcoming exhibition, Franklin Royce?

Franklin Royce is Frank's public name. Stella's never heard anyone call him that in real life before.

Frank comes over to Blue and kisses her on both cheeks. Only if you're very lucky, and if you keep still when I ask you to.

You'll be the lucky one. I'm far too hyperactive to model.

I've no interest in models, he says. He nods towards Stella. Have you met my latest muse?

I thought she was your stepdaughter.

She is. But she also happens to be a dream in front of the camera. Unfussy, almost childlike.

That's because she is a child, says Blue. She turns to Stella. How do you feel about all this?

It isn't a question Stella's been asked before. Frank's interest in taking photographs of her only developed this holiday. I don't mind, she says. It's fun.

There you go then. Your girl loves the limelight.

In school, Stella's not one of the pretty girls. Her face is round and freckled, with a low, square forehead. She isn't particularly tall or thin. The limelight is a place in which she'd never imagined finding herself. Claire, on the other hand, modelled when she was younger. Stella's seen some of the editorials hung up in her grandparents' bathroom.

A few months ago, Stella attended one of Frank's shows. It was full of blurred, bare-skinned women against a blue sky, and those translucent, dusty-looking bubbles that sunlight sometimes creates in a lens. His photographs were printed large enough to take up an entire wall on their own, and people seemed to be able to stand in front of them for hours, just staring. Stella knows her grandparents don't have that much space in their house, or that much patience.

Frank lifts his camera and snaps it a few times at Stella. She isn't sure if he's seriously taking photographs, or if he's performing for Blue.

Jasmine's voice carries over from the veranda. Stella hadn't realised she was there. Will you two stop treating this whole place as your fucking studio?

It was me who paid for this villa, says Frank, and I'll treat it how I like.

Whatever. We're heading into town, right Blue?

Blue pulls her legs out of the pool and stands up. Stella thinks that if she had a camera, she'd take a photograph of Blue right there, on the edge of the pool like that.

You wanna come?

Hell no, calls Jasmine.

It's OK. I'm fine here.

Blue's hair is made up of tight curls that skim the waistline of her bikini bottoms. When she turns to leave, beads of water spray out from the ends and catch the sun.

Neither Blue nor Jasmine has a licence to drive the car that Frank's rented, so they take the old mopeds that belong to the house. Stella hears the exhausts flare and then fizzle as they drive away. She swims for a while. Claire and Frank set up on the veranda and start eating tuna niçoise.

Come try this, calls Claire. Have you been drinking enough water?

The salad has green beans in it, and the water next to Stella's plate has been poured into a pint glass. She takes a sip.

Drink it all, says Claire. Show me you can.

I'm not eight.

No, says Frank. You're eighteen. Now down that pint. Down it.

Stella drinks the entire glass of water in one. She splutters as she finishes, trying not to laugh. By the time she gets around to her salad, Claire and Frank are done eating. Frank gets his camera out and holds it to his eye, twisting the lens very slowly so that it ticks like a clock.

Frank's camera is newly fitted with something called a dream lens, a rare piece of kit that he bought specifically for the intense sunshine of the holiday. A month before, he'd sent the lens to Japan, along with his film camera – purchased for thousands of pounds at an auction the previous year – to be modified to fit.

Stella only knows such details because Frank has told her. Frank is obsessed with his photography equipment. The day before they caught their flight out here, Stella watched him line up his camera, lenses and film canisters in the rectangle of light coming in through his bedroom window before taking a photograph of them on his phone.

I'm shooting the tools I use to shoot, he'd said over his shoulder. How meta.

Stella finishes eating and gathers up the plates to take inside to wash. Something about having Frank around makes her a better daughter, and she can feel it happening. This seems to work the same for Claire too; since she married Frank, she remembers things like how much water Stella's drunk that day.

Stella stacks Frank's plate on top of the rest. He reaches out and puts his hand on her forearm. He's leaning back in his chair with his linen shirt undone, his camera still unzipped from its case. His chest hair is silver, the skin on his bare stomach thick and red-brown.

Jasmine should lay off you, he says, now Blue's here as distraction.

Stella thinks of Blue, standing on the edge of the pool in the midday sun. Maybe, she replies.

That evening all five of them go out for dinner to a restaurant on the beach.

Stella sits at the head of the table, Jasmine and Blue on either side. Jasmine's wearing a baby-pink sundress, and has picked out each of her eyelashes with a lot of mascara. Blue isn't wearing any make-up, but her dress is made of gold sequins that throw rainbows across the drinking glasses. Her bare feet are dirty with red dust, and she has a few long, dark hairs growing out of her toes. On her wrists, she's wearing thick silver jewellery that rings when she moves.

Stop looking at my friend, says Jasmine. It's like, super weird.

Stella feels the inside of her mouth get dry. She pours herself a glass of water from the bottle and takes a sip.

Now, now, says Frank. Don't be jealous.

As the waiter pours Blue's wine, she leans back in her chair and starts speaking to him. Her Spanish is soft and low. The waiter gets his notebook out.

Hey small fry. You want what the grown-ups are having?

Stella nods. I eat everything. There's nothing I don't eat.

My kinda girl.

There's a huge steel dish of paella with wedges of lemon, a pile of calamari, and a platter of tiny green peppers, scorched black and sprinkled with rocks of salt. Blue teaches Stella how to rip the head from a prawn and suck the brains out of it, and use the shell of one mussel as a pincer to pull the flesh from another. For pudding, there are entire lemons that have been scooped out and filled with ice cream, and a plate of purple figs.

You know, says Blue. Every fig you eat still contains the corpse of the wasp that pollinated it.

For real? says Stella.

Jasmine hasn't spoken for almost the entire meal, just moved the rice from one side of her plate to the other. Now, she lifts her napkin to her mouth and spits a chewed fig into it. That's fucking gross, she says.

Blue shakes her head. It's nature, baby. That prawn you just ate spent most of its life nibbling a bunch of parasites off larger sea creatures to keep them clean. What d'you think of that?

Jasmine takes a long pull on her wine. Just stop talking.

Claire and Frank laugh. They like Blue, Stella can tell.

Are you planning to go to university in September? asks Claire.

Jasmine rolls her eyes, as she does every time Claire speaks. Jasmine herself is hoping to go to Sussex, although there's some doubt around whether she'll get the grades.

My first choice is Glasgow, says Blue.

You and Jasmine'll be living at opposite ends of the country, says Frank. How on earth will you cope?

Oh, I'll have a whole new crew by then, says Blue. I won't still be wasting my time with this one.

Everyone laughs at that, apart from Jasmine. Stella laughs so hard she nearly falls off her chair. When the laughter dies down, Jasmine's looking right at her.

Oh yeah? Because you've got so many friends yourself.

Oi, says Blue. Lay off. I'm her friend.

Yeah, says Stella. *She's* my friend.

Jasmine shakes her head. She's just using you to wind me up. Blue and I have been best friends since we were practically babies.

That's what she thinks, says Blue. I'm just in it for the free holidays.

Claire and Frank laugh more. Stella bites down on the insides of her cheeks.

Blue leans forward, catches Stella's eye, and winks. Hey bestie, she says. You wanna split the last fig?

The next day, Stella wakes late. The sun filters through the wooden shutters. A mosquito, fat with her blood, swims lazily around the top of the net. There's no air con in the house, so Stella spent the night thrashing about in the wet heat, re-angling the fan so that it was pointing at her face.

The door opens, and there's Blue, dressed in a pair of fluorescent orange bikini bottoms and a white crop top, her dark nipples just visible underneath. One of her hands is full of cherries, the other full of stones.

Morning lazybones. We're going to the beach.

Me and you?

Yup, and Jazz.

Blue swings the door closed behind her. Woah. These are so cute.

She drops the cherry stones in a small pile on the dresser, and reaches down for a pair of trainers that are peeking out from under Stella's bed. She holds them up to the soles of her feet, then tosses them back down again. Too small, she says.

Blue picks up other items of Stella's clothing from the floor and holds them against herself. Can I borrow this?

Blue pulls the T-shirt over her head. It's green, with little frills at the sleeves. On it is stitched a felt bumble bee and the words *Bee Kind*.

I only ever wear that as pyjamas.

Really? I love it.

The T-shirt is tight on Blue, but in a good way. It rides up to show a strip of stomach, her bellybutton as dark and perfect as the cherries she was eating.

By the time they leave the bedroom, Blue's dressed head to toe in Stella's clothes. She's wearing sunglasses decorated at the edges with plastic daisies, and a pair of stretchy shorts so small for her they look like knickers.

Jasmine's waiting on the sofa, swinging a set of moped keys in her fingers. What the fuck are you wearing? she says.

Blue gives a twirl. Stella knows that most grown women in that outfit would look crazy, but Blue manages to pull it off.

Come on, says Jasmine. We're going.

Stella's coming too.

Seriously?

Blue underlines the slogan on her T-shirt with her finger. Read it and weep, baby, she says.

The first time Stella met Jasmine, Frank had just left Jasmine's mother for hers. It was winter, and they went out for breakfast in a new café that had opened near Stella's school. Stella got a hot chocolate with marsh-mallows that melted and gave a sweet, chemical taste to the milk. Jasmine was wearing foundation so thick her skin looked prosthetic. She looked at her phone under the table the entire time. If Stella closed her eyes, it was almost like Jasmine wasn't there at all.

Come on Jazzy, said Frank. Say something. Say anything.

Claire touched him lightly on the arm. It's OK, don't push it. She'll talk when she's ready.

The bill had to be paid at the counter. When they got up to leave, there were lots of people in the queue. Jasmine and Stella went and stood outside. The wind was cold, and Stella pulled her scarf up around her ears.

Your dad's really nice, said Stella, through the material.

Jasmine was standing with her body facing the road, not looking at Stella. Well your mum's a fucking home-wrecking fucking whore.

She spoke at an even volume, as if she was saying something completely normal, still looking out over the road as the cars went by. Stella didn't reply. The words stayed in her head like an echo, and she couldn't think of anything else.

When Frank and Claire came outside, they all got in the same car. Jasmine was still living in the house Stella lives in now, and Frank was staying in the flat that Claire and Stella had lived in all Stella's life. Frank gave Jasmine a lift home, and she made him drop her off a block from the house.

I don't want you setting her off again, she said, before she climbed out.

Blue swings her leg over the moped, slots the key into the ignition, and slaps the empty part of the seat behind her. Hop on, she says. Let's make this pussy roar.

Blue drives fast. The paths are bumpy and full of sharp turns. Her body feels solid and strong, like hugging a snake. The wind combs Stella's hair. They drive through the pink salt flats, past fields of dry, ploughed earth, pulling over intermittently to let Jasmine catch up. Jasmine's nervous on the moped, whirring along at the speed of the bicycles, looking over her shoulder constantly to check for approaching cars.

It isn't long before they're lost. The beach is small and deserted, with gritty sand. The sea is choppy, mauve jellyfish bobbing like single-use plastic. Blue and Jasmine take their bikini tops off and lean back on the puckered grey rocks to tan.

You're in my light, Jasmine says to Stella, though she isn't.

Once the girls become so hot and thirsty that they have to brave the sea, Jasmine devises a game in which Stella has to paddle around her and Blue in circles to make sure they don't get stung.

Oh please, says Blue. That's practically child labour.

I wasn't planning on paying her.

It's OK, says Stella. I don't mind.

In fact, she doesn't. There's something heroic-sounding about the set-up to her. She'd never been stung by a jellyfish, and doesn't imagine it could hurt that bad. Although Stella sticks to the plan, it's Jasmine that gets stung. Her scream is throaty.

You've got to piss on it, says Blue, back on the sand.

Jasmine is hopping on one foot. That's disgusting, she says. Her eyes are wet with tears and a hot-pink rash has flared up on her ankle.

I swear, says Blue. It neutralises the sting.

Jasmine frowns, but she lifts her ankle. Fine. You do it.

Sorry, babe. I went when we were swimming. Small fry might have something to offer.

Stella sucks her bottom lip.

Go on then, says Jasmine.

Stella squats. It takes a while for the piss to come. She's nervous with them both watching over her like that. Her aim isn't particularly good, and she only manages to get a little bit on Jasmine's sting. The rest splashes up around her ankles and across Jasmine's shins. Jasmine squeezes her eyes shut and retches.

There, says Blue. Wasn't that good bonding?

Back at the villa, Frank and Claire have left a note on the table saying they've gone into town for dinner, but there's fish from the market in the fridge that the girls can barbeque.

Blue enrols Stella to help. She says she's seen a bunch of samphire down by the lagoon. Stella doesn't know what that is, but she follows. They walk barefoot in silence. Geckos scuttle in the dry stone walls, and the yellow grass creaks. Blue teaches Stella how to pick the more tender stalks of samphire by snapping them to check the thickness of their stems. They collect them in a sand-castle bucket that Blue found in the garage. When they have enough, they leave the bucket on a low wall and go swimming. The lagoon's warm, and only as deep as Stella's waist. The sun sinks into it as they swim, leaving the sky and the water the same orange-pink.

Back in the shallows, they stand to walk out. The bottom is smooth, slimy clay, and Stella feels her feet sink into it with every step. The swim has shifted Blue's swimming costume, revealing the lighter shade of skin beneath. Water gathers over her body in droplets and runs down her legs. On the thin slip of sand at the shore of the lagoon, Blue carves the words *Stella & Blue 4eva* with a stick.

In the kitchen, they boil the samphire and chop it fine with other ingredients like capers and red onion to make a relish. There's a barbeque on the veranda, and Blue lines fillets of white fish over the coals. The flood-lights are on in the pool, and the water looks like a huge turquoise crystal.

Jasmine comes out and sits on the veranda, swatting at her ankles to get rid of the mosquitos. She's wearing a beach kaftan made of sheer cotton, and the outline of her bikini can be seen underneath. Her body has wide, soft curves like a Kardashian, whereas Blue is gangly and narrow, with the bones sticking out in her shoulders. Blue serves the fish, and Stella spoons the relish. Blue and Jasmine drink wine.

Blue talks for a long time about one of the boys she's dating back home, and Stella can't understand half of what she's saying. He's a total stoner, but he goes down on me whenever I want.

After the fish is gone, Stella takes a scoop more relish and eats it plain off the spoon.

What d'you reckon, small fry?

Most delicious thing I've ever tasted. Zingy!

Glad you like.

Stella almost takes another spoonful, but changes her mind. Let's save the rest for Mum and Frank. I want them to try it.

Jasmine sniffs. They'll be full up on posh shit.

Like what?

Lobster, probably.

A vibe, says Blue. Maybe I should start fucking your dad.

Gross, says Jasmine. Please don't.

Blue licks the length of her knife. I'd fuck anyone for a lobster.

The following day, Frank drives all five of them out to the edge of the island where the caves have created little swimming pools from the sea. The rocks are sand-coloured and craterous from the spray. Blue and Jasmine swim off to explore the caves, while Frank gets his camera out and waits on the rocks above for the sun to move a fraction. Stella stays below, trying to forget the camera is on her, and watches Claire, who's laying out towels in a sheltered section of the cave for everyone to sit on. She's brought a cool box filled with water bottles and beers, as well as a few bags of salted almonds. The freckles have come out on her face, some of them joining together into age spots. She's wearing a black swimming costume with a green sarong tied around her waist, and the soft skin on the underside of her arms has concertinaed into lots of tiny wrinkles.

The rock edge of the pool is covered in sea urchins, so Frank swims next to Claire as she climbs in, his face close to the water, pointing out the safest spots to step. The sea is teal, and Stella can see a bike wedged in the sand at the bottom.

What did you guys eat last night? asks Stella, once they're out.

Frank is wearing expensive sunglasses, and the lenses blink in the sun. Lots of things, he says. Tapas.

But what? Specifically. Tell me every single thing.

Claire laughs.

Alright, says Frank. Um. We had some big fat prawns, Spanish omelette, patatas bravas.

Those marinated anchovies that I like. We had lots of those.

There was bread and aioli, and some olives.

We had an aubergine thing as well. And some delicious little croquettes.

So no lobster?

Lobster? says Claire. Not that I can think of. Why d'you ask?

No reason, says Stella. Just wondering.

Jasmine and Blue get back a little after that. Jasmine sits down with a beer while Blue climbs up over the rocks. Stella's noticed that Blue is always moving. Even when she sunbathes, she jitters one of her ankles, or ties little plaits into her hair.

Look, shouts Blue. This is the perfect place to jump.

Stella isn't so sure. It's high where Blue is standing, and the rock curves outward, so that if Blue didn't push herself off far enough she could scrape her body on the way down.

Jazz, get your ass up here. You too, small fry.

Even getting over to the platform is a little scary, and both Stella and Jasmine have to use their hands to support themselves as they climb. There's just enough space for all three girls to stand side by side on the ledge. The rock bulges beneath them, the sea so far off it looks solid. A cloud passes over the sun, and the water flashes black. It occurs to Stella that Jasmine might push her off, and she shifts slightly towards Blue.

Below, Claire and Frank stand to watch. Be careful, Claire calls.

On three, says Blue. OK? Three. Two. One.

It's only Blue that jumps. Jasmine and Stella stay standing. Blue's body is in the air for whole minutes before the sea swallows her whole. Stella watches the white foam spit on the surface and waits.

Fuck, says Jasmine.

Blue comes up whooping. Come on, pussies, she shouts.

Jasmine has her arms folded across her chest. I'm not doing it.

She starts to make her way back down the rock. Stella stands on the platform, contemplating. Underneath her, Blue treads water and waves. The sea sloshes lightly against the rocks. Stella thinks about how if she died when she jumped, it would be all Blue's fault, and their names would be tied together forever.

Stella jumps. The bulge of the rock passes so close to her body she can hear it, like a bus driving too fast down the street. Someone screams, probably her mother. The air feels hard, and the surface of the water even harder. When Stella comes up, she's shaken, certain that her organs have swapped places inside her body. Blue swims to her.

You good?

Stella's panting so loud she can barely hear. She grins. Yeah, she says, between pants. That was great. That was so, so great.

Blue puts her thumb in the air so that the others can see. Claire's had her hands over her face, and she takes them down.

Again? says Stella, though she doesn't want to.

In the car on the way back to the villa, the seats are so hot they burn. Stella puts her head on Blue's shoulder and closes her eyes.

What shall we eat tonight? says Frank. I can drive via the shop.

It's Blue's last night, says Jasmine. We were planning to go out.

Stella lifts her face to Blue's. No. That went way too fast.

Light comes through the sunroof and shows a faint, dark moustache on Blue's upper lip. Only a few weeks ago, Stella noticed her own in the zoom-in mirror that Frank has in the bathroom, and used his razor to shave it off.

Come with us, says Blue. You're invited. Isn't she, Jasmine?

Jasmine doesn't respond, and Frank coughs to fill the silence.

See, says Blue. I told you she'd be cool with it.

Frank laughs then, and so does Claire. Stella wonders if Blue was born exceptional, or if it's the kind of thing that happens gradually.

At the villa, Stella sits on the veranda with the adults while Jasmine and Blue shower and get ready to go out. It's almost like before Blue arrived: Claire leafing through a book, Frank loading a new film into his camera. He puts the previous canister carefully into his bag, and lets out a long, low whistle.

There's some great shots on that sucker, he says.

Quickly, Stella prays that the best photographs are of her.

Stell, says Claire. You'll be careful tonight, won't you? Those girls are adults. You don't have to do the things they do.

I know, Mum.

A shout comes from inside the house. Hey, small fry. Come try this. I think it'll suit you.

The dress is made of velour in a muted gold colour. Stella puts it on in her bedroom, and Blue tightens the spaghetti straps by tying them in knots on Stella's shoulders. On Blue, the dress would have been shin-length, but on Stella it trails the floor, and she has to lift it every time she takes a step.

Guapa.

What's that?

It means gorgeous.

Stella looks in the mirror.

Go ahead, says Blue. Play dumb. Act like you don't know.

I didn't know! I'd never heard that word before.

I mean you're acting like you don't know you're gorgeous.

Frank drives the girls into town, pulling into a bus stop to drop them off. He passes Stella a roll of notes through the window, to pay for dinner.

What about me? says Jasmine.

I was getting to you.

The cobbled streets are strung with fairy lights, and the tiny church is floodlit. Lots of men run their eyes over Blue as she walks. Stella follows directly behind and pretends it's her that the men are looking at. When they come to the restaurant, Jasmine picks a table that's set up on the street outside. The moon is big and yellow in the gap between the buildings, and Blue orders red wine that comes in a carafe with short, stubby glasses.

Have a sip, says Blue.

Stella shakes her head and shivers. I've tried wine before. It's horrible.

It's not how it tastes, small fry. It's how it makes you *feel*.

Blue pours her a glass, and Jasmine picks it up and drinks. Hey, says Stella. That was for me.

When Jasmine puts the glass back on the table, it's empty. You're twelve years old. Remember?

How could I forget.

Jasmine laughs, for the first time Stella's ever heard. It feels nice.

Blue orders an entire fish that comes on an oval platter, swimming in its own juices. She pops the eyeball out with her fork and places it carefully in the middle of Stella's empty plate.

That's your dinner. If you're good, you can have the other one after.

I know you're joking.

I'm deadly serious.

Stella picks the eyeball off her plate. In her fingers, it feels like the balls of polystyrene that had protected Frank's new lens when it arrived in the post. Stella tosses the eyeball into her mouth and swallows.

No one speaks for a moment. Stella worries she's done the wrong thing. Then Blue slips low into her chair, throws her head back and laughs and laughs. I fucking love this kid, she says.

Stella feels her body float upwards, a little off the seat. Jasmine cuts a fillet away from the fish and places it on

Stella's plate. Here, she says. To get the taste out. I'll get you some water as well.

The girls begin to eat. Blue and Jasmine talk about learning to drive, which Jasmine is doing and Blue is avoiding.

Dad took me out to practise once, says Jasmine. I guess he thought it was a good opportunity for bonding.

A good opportunity for mansplaining, says Blue.

Literally. The only person he was bonding with was himself.

Like that's necessary.

Jasmine nods. He's a shit driver, too.

Fuck driving anyway, says Blue. I'd rather get driven.

That's probably best for everyone, pipes up Stella, thinking of her ride on the moped.

Jasmine laughs at that, too.

They're midway through the meal when Blue waves at someone. Stella looks over her shoulder to see a man a few tables away.

This guy's been eyeing me for ages, says Blue, not breaking her smile.

The man has hair that looks matted on purpose, and there's a guitar propped against his chair. He's fit, says Jasmine.

He's alright, says Blue.

Yeah, says Stella. Nothing special.

What do you know about it, small fry? says Blue. She calls the man over. You fancy buying us a drink? she says, when he arrives.

How old is she? says the man. His accent is maybe French or Italian.

That's Stella. She's nineteen.

And your name?

Blue.

OK. Now I'm sure you're lying.

Blue reaches over and pulls the empty chair back from their table. We drink vodka, she says. Vodka and orange.

What are you doing? asks Jasmine, once the man is inside the restaurant, standing at the bar.

What does it look like? You said you fancied him.

I said he was fit. It's different.

Is it?

The man comes back with a round tray. He puts the drinks down on the table. Jasmine moves Stella's glass next to hers. This time, Stella doesn't protest. The man sits down. He tells them his name is Nico.

We have a question for you, Nico, says Blue.

Go on.

D'you think there's a difference between fancying someone and thinking they're fit?

Under her make-up, Jasmine goes pink. Nico doesn't notice; he's looking at Blue. My English might not be good enough for this question, he says.

Just answer. We're having a debate.

Nico picks up his guitar and starts plucking at the strings. What's *fit*?

It means hot, says Blue. Sexy, attractive. It's what Jasmine thinks of you.

Jasmine blushes even more then. She has her eyes on her empty plate, and she looks to Stella like she might start to cry. Nico is smiling a little, amused.

So, what's your answer?

I'd say they're the same.

Blue grins. That means you're with me.

Nico looks at Blue, and she looks back. The evening is balmy, and their faces are shimmering. Stella thinks that the sounds coming from the guitar are sort of tinny, perhaps out of tune. That look lasts a long time.

The screech of Jasmine's chair against the paving makes Stella jump. She has to run to catch her.

Are you OK?

I'm fine. Leave me alone.

That was kinda unfair.

What was?

You know.

Jasmine stops. They're at the bottom of the street by now. The fairy lights have run out and things are a shade darker. Jasmine's face is mostly covered by her hair, but Stella can see that her mascara is running.

I'm used to it, she says. I'm never the first choice.

Blue arrives then. She's jogged down, and her breathing's loud. I've always wanted to do a runner, she says.

Jasmine wipes the mascara from under her eyes with her index finger. Fuck's sake, she says, turning to make her way back to the restaurant.

At their table, Nico has gone. Perhaps Blue sent him away, or perhaps he was simply afraid of being lumbered with their bill. Stella hopes it is the former. She pulls Frank's money from inside her trainer, and leaves the lot in the middle of the table. Neither Blue nor Jasmine make signs of contributing.

The taxi ride home is taken in silence. Stella rolls the window down, sticks her head out, and watches white stars run through the sky like streamers.

At the villa, Frank and Claire are in bed already, and the girls sit out on the veranda. There's a box of cigarettes on the table, so Jasmine and Blue help themselves to a couple. After Jasmine lights the cigarettes, she uses the matches to light the candles on the table. The girls' faces flicker.

Isn't it past your bedtime? says Jasmine.

Blue takes a drag of her cigarette. Can you put your insecurity on hold for like, five minutes?

Fuck off, Blue.

We all know it's not small fry you're pissed off with, or me.

Jasmine doesn't reply to that. Stella can see the Milky Way behind her head.

It's not even Claire, says Blue. It's your arsehole of a dad.

Jasmine keeps refusing to meet Blue's eye. The ash falls from the end of her cigarette onto the table and scatters.

He spent ten years of his marriage sleeping with Claire, says Blue. He clean broke your mum's heart. She can't get out of bed for weeks at a time, and he's out here with his new wife and his flash camera. He's an arsehole, Jazz. He's a fucking arsehole. Say it with me.

He's an arsehole. He's a fucking arsehole.

Jasmine stands up and goes into the house. Stella cranes her neck, but the lights are off all through the villa. When Jasmine comes back, Frank's camera bag is slung over her shoulder.

No, says Stella.

Jasmine takes the steps down from the veranda. Stella stands up and follows, as does Blue. The cool air opens around them, and Stella's eyes adjust as she walks.

Throw it, says Blue. Let it go.

Blue's enjoying this, Stella can tell. There's something like laughter in her voice. That camera's worth thousands, says Stella. Think of the films. They'll be ruined.

The splash is big enough to set the sensors off. The pool lights up to show Frank's bag sinking to the bottom. It quivers gently as it hits the tiles, its strap settling around it like a rosary.

Fuck, says Jasmine.

Blue laughs. I didn't think you were actually gonna do it.

I'll get it, says Stella. I'll get it now. It might be OK.

Nah. Blue lies her hand on Stella's shoulder. It's over. That camera's fucked.

No one says anything for a while. Stella can feel her pulse in the ends of her fingers, all up her neck. A bat sweeps down from the sky, drinks a sip of water from the pool, and flies off into the dark.

Alright, says Blue. Let's get you kids to bed. That's enough excitement for one night.

Stella barely sleeps at all. It's just past nine when she hears Frank's voice, slightly raised, through the shutters. What the, he says.

In a short space of time, everyone's out on the veranda. Stella supposed that staying in her room would look guilty, and it seems that Blue and Jasmine thought that too. By this point, Frank is already in the pool.

What is it? calls Claire. She looks at Stella, and Stella looks away.

In the pool, Frank splutters as he surfaces. Blue chews on her nails.

My god, says Claire. Is that your camera?

Frank swims with his bag held above the surface. In her mind, Stella sees the water seeping into all the round outlines of the buttons, the ridges where the dream lens has been carved to fit, the film canisters sloshing.

Frank climbs out of the pool and walks back to the veranda. Drops fly off him, and the wet camera slaps at his chest. He passes by Stella, Claire and Blue, until he's standing in front of Jasmine. His face is a strange colour, like something cooked. He leans very close to Jasmine, and she squints back at him. She stands a foot shorter than him, her head angled upwards. It's like that for what feels like hours: nose-to-nose, both shaking, silent but for Frank's ragged breaths. A single tear runs down Jasmine's cheek. The sound of the camera dripping slows to a rhythm.

It was me, says Stella. She has the same feeling she had when she ate the fish eye. It was me, she says again.

Jasmine and Blue look at Stella. Jasmine is crying more now. Frank lowers himself slowly into a chair. The thick skin on his belly makes narrow rolls, and he hangs his head low over them.

What? says Claire.

Stella turns and runs through the house. In her bedroom, Blue's velour dress is a loop on the floor. On the dresser, the cherry stones have lost their shine. Stella crawls into bed, pulls her knees up beneath her chin, and waits.

Some hours later, Stella wakes to Blue shaking her gently. Small fry. Hey, I'm outta here.

In the airless garage, Stella climbs into the car. She didn't see Frank on the way through the house, but Claire is sat in the driver's seat, next to Jasmine. Blue's in the back with Stella, her suitcase jammed into the footwell, her legs folded on either side. No one says a word as they drive. The day's so hot the tarmac on the roads is melting. The whole car smells like Blue: coconut oil and Hawaiian Tropic. Stella watches Claire in the wing mirror. It's clear from her eyes that she's been crying.

The drive to the port takes fifteen minutes. When they arrive, Claire waits with the car while Stella and Jasmine walk Blue to the ferry. The boat is huge and white, chugging black smoke into the cobalt sky. The girls stand on the concrete jetty to say their goodbyes, their shadows long and thin in the afternoon sun.

You're pretty badass, small fry, you know that?

Stella shoves her hands deep into the pockets of her shorts. Thanks.

Behind Blue, the edges of the jetty ripple in the heat. There's a slope set up for boarding, and a man checking tickets. He waves Blue over. The boat's scheduled to leave any minute. It'll take Blue to the mainland, where she'll catch her flight back to London.

Well, says Blue. It's been real.

She pulls Jasmine and Stella into a hug, and they stand like that for a while, sticky against each other. Stella can feel her heartbeat pressed up to Blue's body.

Jasmine and Stella stay a little too far apart after Blue walks away, leaving space for her to change her mind. Instead, the ramp lifts and the boat starts to pull out of the port. After a minute or so, Blue appears on the flat roof of the ferry and stands with her hands on the railings, a black silhouette against the wide sky. Stella waves and waves as Blue gets smaller. When the ferry is unintelligible from the other boats in the distance, Stella and Jasmine turn back to the car park.

Hey. Thanks, by the way.

Stella slows, uses her hand to shield her face, looks at Jasmine and nods.

Through the car windscreen, Stella can see her mother fanning herself with a map of the island. Shotgun, says Stella.

Jasmine doesn't fight her, only gets into the back seat without a word. Stella stands for a moment in the heat, looking out at the horizon, before cracking open the passenger door and climbing in.

The Bread

The day after my abortion, I mixed the ingredients for a loaf of bread. I'm not usually interested in baking, but I had an urge to follow instructions. The mixture felt warm and loose, almost bodily, like sticking my fingers inside a stomach.

As a teenager, I had a lot of sex without contraception. I thought it made me seem aloof not to ask the boys I slept with to put a condom on. I was always trying to come across as aloof. Sometimes I got the morning-after pill, other times I risked it. The boys never called to check.

Over time, I began to assume I was barren. I could make myself cry if I thought about it for too long. I kept having unprotected sex whenever I got the opportunity. I didn't want a baby. More, I craved the drama of an unplanned pregnancy. I'd imagine meeting the father in a greasy spoon to tell him; we'd eat buttered white toast from a rack, and I'd look stressed but beautiful in my school uniform.

On the bus home from the clinic, I researched bread recipes. I was wearing a nappy under my skirt that made a dense puffing noise as I sat down. When my little brother stopped wearing nappies, my mother laid a sheet of plastic over his mattress that crackled in the night. She was attentive to him when we were young, because of the baby she'd lost before he was born. She and my father had planted a rose bush for the baby in the back garden. I was four. That's my sister, I told our neighbour, shouting over the fence.

My pregnancy was by a man I'd met on the last night of a music festival. We didn't visit a greasy spoon because I didn't have his number to invite him. I couldn't remember his first name. What I did remember was that we'd used a condom. I found the gold wrapper in my puffer jacket seven weeks later, when I dug around to check. I was angry at the lack of logic as much as anything else.

The bus picked up speed down a dual carriageway. I felt fine. It slowed again as we hit the suburbs, and the cramps started. I looked at the dense green hedges and the clean bonnets of parked cars, I looked at the sun. I thought of all the lives I might find myself in, and squinted. The cramps rose as we hit the city centre. I was thirsty. I wanted to drink from the bottle belonging to the stranger sitting next to me. Can I have a sip of that? I said.

He shook his head.

When I was six weeks pregnant and didn't know it, I got a call from my friend Eliza. She calls me most days. Do you ever worry that nothing you do matters? she said, when I answered. She worked in the biggest shopping centre in the country.

Hardly ever, I replied. I worry more that everything I do does. The pressure of it might be slowly killing me.

You think that's why you've been feeling ill?

Probably, I said.

Around this time, my phone started trying to sell me Clearblue pregnancy tests. The advert showed a pair of hands cradling a white stick with a blue end. On the stick was a dull, grey screen. Over the course of the advert, the word *pregnant* appeared on the screen, emerging gradually as if rising to the surface of a pond. Sometimes, because of the way I held my phone, I'd mistake the hands for my own. I remember that the fingernails were freshly manicured, square and pink with bright white tips.

When I finally caved and bought a test, I didn't buy Clearblue. I chose the cheap ones that came in a two-pack and showed red lines rather than the actual word. My fingernails were bitten down to the beds. Still, both tests came back positive. The algorithm was more perceptive about my body than I was.

I tried to find meaning. I decided that the man from the music festival and I must have had a deeper connection than I'd felt at the time, and this was the way I'd been notified. I saw him on the tube about a week after I found out. He was facing away from me. At last, I thought, someone to tell me what to do.

When he turned around, it wasn't him at all.

I'd read on an online forum that some bakeries are happy to donate a little of their starter to amateurs. In sourdough baking, a starter is used in place of conventional yeast to help the bread rise. When I got off the bus, I walked to the bakery a few blocks from my street instead of going straight home as I was supposed to. With each step I could feel it leaking out of me.

I wondered what my chances were of actually meeting the man on the tube. I wondered what my chances were of getting pregnant while using a condom. I looked up the latter online. When used correctly, condoms are

98 per cent effective. This means 2 out of 100 women will get pregnant while using one. Or is it that if the same woman has protected sex 100 times, 2 of those times will lead to pregnancy?

The woman behind the counter smiled when I asked for the starter. She went into the back to get it. I could feel a gradual building of pressure in my lower body, and there was a vivid white light behind my eyelids. I offered to buy a brownie, since the starter was free. I'd read on the forum that this was the polite thing to do.

The woman gave me the brownie in a paper bag, the starter in a plastic pot. The loaves behind her head began to slide. The white light was obscuring around a third of my vision. Good luck, she said. A sourdough starter's no different to a baby, really. Feed it, burp it, give it lots of love.

Eliza called me as I was leaving the clinic. I've found this underwear set in Victoria's Secret, she said.

Victoria's Secret use prison labour, I said.

I was thinking of stealing it anyway.

Stealing harms the people on the lowest level first, I said. You could get an employee fired. She might have children to feed.

You're fun today. I'll look up your horoscope.

I just got an abortion.

Eliza's voice went to a whisper. Oh shit, she said. Of course.

I made it home from the bakery very slowly. As soon as I got through my front door, I sank to my knees and crawled up the stairs into bed. When I woke it was early evening, and the pain was extraordinary. I stayed very still. I thought of an undulating graph drawn on a whiteboard. I thought of grey waves on a shingle beach. I thought of breathing nitrous oxide from a balloon.

I met the man on the last night of the festival, by a stall selling chips and onion rings. I didn't fancy him as much as I pretended to myself that I did. The man's tent was slightly larger than the one I was sharing with Eliza, though the exact same brand. I hadn't showered in four days. My vagina smelt like prawn cocktail crisps. I left straight after, and bought a hot chocolate in a polystyrene cup. The teenage boy at the stall told me he hadn't slept the entire weekend, not even for a minute. His smile was massive and unruly against the pastel sky.

On the day before my abortion, I took a cup of tea out to the garden. My garden is small and green, sectioned off by a low wall covered in creepers. There is a broken terracotta pot in the far corner, and lots of fresh, healthy weeds between the cracks in the paving stones. My flat is a rental, so I don't usually waste my time with gardening, but that afternoon I noticed that a tiny flower – pale purple on a long, bright stalk – was starting to shrivel in the heat. I took my tea over to it and poured some of the liquid into the ground. I thought of my sister, the rose bush.

By evening, the purple flower was stronger. I gave it more tea. I thought of a leather jacket I'd seen in a club a few years ago, with white letters sewn across the back: *I was atheist until I realised I am God.* I thought of how I'd forgotten to buy sanitary towels in the supermarket, and would have to pick some up on my way to the clinic in the morning.

Sourdough is a three-day process. On the first day you feed the starter, on the second day you make the dough, and on the third, you bake it. I used equal parts flour and water for the feed. The smell coming off as I stirred was tangy and over-sweet, like the mouldy underside of an orange. There you go, I said, aloud.

I didn't change out of the nappy until the middle of the night. I'd forgotten to do it before then, or perhaps I'd been afraid to look. I was woken by the child next door playing video games, machine guns purring through the walls. It was 3 a.m. and I had no texts. In the bathroom, I found a lot of blood and large clots. The metal smell hit me, and I turned around to throw up into the toilet.

After I brushed my teeth, I put the nappy in the bin and stuck a clean sanitary towel inside a pair of clean knickers. I thought of the fingernails in the Clearblue advert, and considered this a fresh beginning. Back in bed, I looked up my weekly horoscope on my phone. I read that there was a new moon in my sign. According to my horoscope, this was a good time to set intentions for the year, and to leave the past behind. Be assured, I read, that the universal plan is unfolding.

On the day after my abortion, I stretched and folded the dough every two hours to help with the structure of the loaf. The process was like kneading, only gentler. Before I started, I watched five YouTube tutorials for technique. I rehearsed the movements in the air with my hands.

In the first two-hour slot between folds, I went out to the garden with a cup of tea. I was in a lot less pain than the day before, but still I had waves of dizziness and nausea. I brought with me three ginger nuts from the cupboard; I'd been told by the doctor that ginger could help. I put one of the biscuits in my mouth, felt it break into a paste and slip down my throat. I was pleased to be told what to do, and to do it.

Eliza texted me four photographs of herself in the underwear she'd stolen from Victoria's Secret. She was standing in the changing rooms. She must have hidden the underwear under all her clothes and walked out right after. There was a photograph of a model wearing a pair of angel wings hung on the back wall, reflected in the mirror to the left of Eliza's head.

In the second two-hour slot, I took a long shower. The water around my feet ran rusty. I lowered myself to the wet floor, placing my head between my folded legs and my knees by my temples. My back was curved against the sliding door, my eyes squeezed, the underside of my lids deep red. I sat like that a while, water pouring down. When I came to I felt embarrassed, then self-indulgent, then livid. I got up, wrapped myself in a dressing gown, and stormed towards my bedroom. I caught the sleeve of the dressing gown on the handle of the bathroom door. My shoulder crunched in the socket. I freed myself, beat the door with my clenched fists and howled.

The nurse had asked if I wanted the screen to be turned away during the ultrasound. I'd said yes. The room was very dark. The light coming from the screen was blue on the nurse's face. I worried that I'd hear the heartbeat, but I didn't. I suppose she'd turned the volume down.

In the final two-hour slot, I fell asleep on the sofa. I had a new-found capacity for sleeping. I woke to my phone, thinking it was the alarm I'd set to remind myself about the bread. It was Eliza.

Can you reply to those photos I sent? I don't know which to post.

I'm busy, I said. I'm baking.

Baking what?

Bread.

Have you thought about the pun?

It took me a moment to get it. When I did, I hung up.

In the bathroom, my sanitary towel had bled over again. There was a dull, low pain. I was supposed to be keeping track of the bleeding, but I didn't know how much was too much. I ripped the pad out, tossed it, and took two painkillers, holding my mouth to the tap.

According to the online recipe I was following, a finished loaf turns out best if it's shaped twice, half an hour apart. The first shape is called the pre-shape. I floured the counter, floured my hands, and turned the dough out. There was a soft, powdery smell. I leant into it, and started. The bread was big and soft with air, like the underside of a breast. I was gentle with the shaping; my touch was more of a stroke, a coaxing.

Eliza posted the second photograph of herself in the underwear on Instagram. I thought the third was better, but I didn't tell her. All Eliza really did on socials was post thirst traps. She told me once that this was the only way she felt she could claim power over her own body. I suspected that really it was her way of reminding herself how much power she already had. She was thin with boobs, and only fucked men who loved her.

After shaping the dough a final time, I floured a clean bowl that I'd lined with a tea towel and nestled the bread inside. After, washing my hands, I noticed a white crust under each of my fingernails. I didn't scrub them away. I liked that the bread had left its mark on my body.

The following week, I heard a horoscope columnist on the radio. I was still bleeding, though only a little. He explained that a written horoscope will avoid specifics wherever possible, so that individual readers can shape the descriptions to fit themselves. Because the readings are vague, and because most people's weeks are a mix of good and bad, those who look for confirmations of their horoscope will inevitably find them. The readings are a careful marriage of chance and logic.

Two days after my abortion, I baked the bread for half an hour. It was mid-morning. The smell was of toast, though denser. I lifted the loaf from the rack and turned it in my oven gloves. I don't know what I had expected to feel. Authority, perhaps. I didn't feel that. I had baked a fine loaf of sourdough, but that was all. When the heat started burning through my oven gloves, I put the bread down on a wood board and watched the steam filter up, out of the window.

Today's Square

We've been in lockdown three months. Ma's taken to
sleeping way into the afternoon, then staying awake until
five o'clock in the morning scrolling the news on her
phone. I've taken to crossing the days off the calendar
with my pink gel pen as they pass, using my jelly ruler
to make the lines perfect. In the little square labelled 24
June, which is today, Ma's written *Tenerife 15.30*. Ma's
handwriting always reminds me of the popular girls in
school, who draw big, round letters and dot their i's with
tiny circles.

I've been on holiday just once before. I was five or six,
and I only remember it in snatches. In one memory, I'm

in the shallows of the sea with my hands dug down into the sand and my eyes just above the surface of the water, like a crocodile on the hunt. In another, a man comes to our table at dinner with a cone of roses and Ma buys me one, stands it up in my water glass while we eat. In my last, the aeroplane tilts towards the sun and ovals of gold light slide over the passengers, who squint their eyes against it.

Ma's saved for the last four years so we could afford a second holiday. Before the company she worked for announced liquidation due to the virus, she used to get paid overtime in cash. She stored it in a plastic wallet at the back of the cupboard, behind the box of teabags.

At the weekends, Ma liked to get the plastic wallet out and count its contents. The day she found she'd saved enough, she swore more times than I'd ever heard.

Fuck off, she said. You're fucking joking.

She was using her phone to look up the flights; her laptop's been broken for ever.

I'm doing it, baby, she said. Fuck it, I'm fucking doing it.

Her thumbs tapped at the screen for a while. Fuck, she said after. Fuckedy fuck.

For a 15.30 flight, we'd have to leave the flat at 10.30 in the morning. Ma mapped it all out for me. There was the bus to the station, and then the train to the airport, and then the shuttle to the terminal. There was bag drop and security, then there was sometimes a long wait in the terminal, then a queue at the gate to board the plane. I was excited for every part, even the waiting.

I keep looking at the clock: 10.30 comes and goes. I cross out the square on the calendar with Ma's writing in it, even though I usually save this for evening, when I'm absolutely certain that the day is done.

I make myself some instant noodles: sticky rather than soupy, which is how I'm starting to prefer them. At one o'clock, Ma's still sleeping. I open the curtains in the living room. The light floods in and bleaches the walls. It's nice out.

A few years ago, a man fell from our floor and died. After that, restrictors were put on all the windows, so we can only get them open a crack. I push the window as far as it will go and stand in the middle of the room, imagining the new air filtering in all around me.

Ma said we wouldn't still be in lockdown by now. She said it more than once. When all this started, I used to ask most days.

We're still going to Tenerife, right? I'd say.

Yes, baby. Don't you worry about that. Wash your hands properly, get between the fingers. Your mask can come off now.

Later, she stopped replying. I knew that meant no, but I kept asking anyway, just in case.

The day she paid for our flights and hotel, Ma took the money out of the plastic wallet and deposited it at the bank. There was still a little left, and whenever she worked overtime she'd add more, so that we had spending money for the trip.

A few weeks ago, when Ma's card bounced doing the food order, she took the plastic wallet down from the cupboard and left for the bank. I understood for certain then that Tenerife was no longer happening. I stopped asking for good, after that.

It gets closer and closer to 15.30. I panic when I think we're going to miss our plane, and then I remember. An idea comes to me, and I start on it before I can persuade myself not to.

I get up and go to the door. I put on my mask and a pair of black rubber gloves from the cardboard box. I flick the door onto the latch.

The hallway is silent. In the beginning, people played music out their windows, and shouts carried up from the flats below. These days, there's nothing. I go to the stairwell and look out the vent. All the equipment is there on the platform, same as always. Way below, there are two police officers standing on the green, the hi-vis panels on their bulletproof vests winking in the sun.

I slot my body through the vent and climb out onto the scaffolding. The air tastes like cucumber, and I can feel the wind stroking my neck. I keep low to the wooden platform, crawling along it on my hands and knees out of fear of being seen. There's no barrier to keep me from falling, only a long steel bar that I'd be small enough to slip under.

The morning after the man fell from his window, I saw the police tape when I left for school. The body had been taken away, but they'd not yet got around to cleaning up the blood.

In the beginning, Ma and I would go down to the green to do star jumps and burpees in the fresh air. We'd take the stairs up after, all twenty-one flights, just to make it last longer. The stairwell goes down one side of the building, with a long vent in the concrete, so it's sort of like being outside.

The tiredness would hit me about halfway, and I'd have to stop for a break. Ma wouldn't let me touch the banister while I rested, not even with my gloves on. She'd stand with me while I got my breath back, holding out my inhaler in case I needed it.

We can get the lift the rest of the way, she'd say. Don't push yourself too hard, baby.

I'd always refuse. While I breathed, I'd look out the vent and watch the builders on the scaffolding up the side of our block. They were some of the only people still working, apart from the NHS Heroes. I guess because they worked outside, they were told to keep going. They had a crackling radio, and they'd sing along to it as they swung bags of sand across to one another, or abseiled from one temporary platform to the next.

At the time, they were the only people I saw apart from Ma. None of them wore masks, and their faces were expressive as cartoons. I felt my whole body relax when I looked at them; my pulse would gently slow.

A few weeks ago, the builders stopped coming. They left their equipment piled up on one of the platforms. It was the highest platform, on the same level as our flat. The builders had taken the things that were more expensive, like the radio and the power tools, but they'd left the rest. There were bags of sand, orange trays of screws, planks of wood. There was even a cup of tea, half-drunk.

The bags of sand have been tied at the top. I grab one of the knots and pull it towards me. The bag's heavier than I'd imagined, and it takes three wrenches to get it to the end of the platform. Once there, I tuck my hands under the hessian and attempt to lift the bag up and over the concrete wall, so I can roll it through the vent and into the stairwell. I'm squatting with my back to the drop, unsteady with the effort.

The sound the bag makes when it lands on the stairs is dense and short. I freeze, hunched over on the platform, waiting for someone to come out and catch me.

The second bag is easier, because by now I know what I'm doing, and harder, because I've used up most of my energy on the first. When it's over, I have to lie down on the platform and concentrate on my breathing for a while. I envisage the clean, new air filling my lungs and pumping all through my body.

I use the same lift-and-roll technique to get the bags of sand up the stairs. It's only half a flight, but it takes me about twenty minutes of straining. Once I'm on level ground, dragging the bags through the front door is easy. I leave them in the hallway while I hang my mask up, throw away my gloves, and get my inhaler from the drawer in the kitchen. I spend a while on the sofa, just breathing.

I check for Ma, who's still asleep, before I drag the bags across the hall and into the living room. I use a kitchen knife to slit them. The sand is dark and gritty, but it will have to do. I scatter it about with my hands, breaking apart the wetter clumps as I go. When I'm sure it's packed to the edges, I use the broom to get an even spread.

When Ma booked our trip, it was on two conditions. I couldn't miss one day of school all year, and I'd ask for extra homework tasks at the end of every week. We couldn't afford to go away in the summer holidays, because everything got so much more expensive then.

Homeschool lasted a little longer than the star jumps and burpees, but once my teacher got sick and stopped sending videos, Ma said she didn't have the energy to keep it up on her own.

Every week, I leave the flat just once, to collect our food order from the lift. Ma would never have allowed me to do this earlier in the lockdown, but these days she's usually sleeping when it comes. The delivery person rings the bell and I buzz them up. They put the order in the lift, and when the doors open, I take it out.

Recently, the delivery man came up in the lift with our order. He must have been new at the job. He was wearing a blue cap and a knitted scarf across his face.

Stay back, he said.

I didn't move at all. I couldn't even if I'd wanted to. The man put the order on the floor outside the lift. He pressed the button and the steel doors slid closed behind him. I stayed out in the hall for up to a minute, staring at the box of food, before I picked it up and brought it inside.

Every time I go out to collect the food order, I go to the stairwell to check the builders' equipment. I keep expecting them to come back for it, but every week it's still there. Part of me likes seeing it, because it means I haven't missed them. Another part of me is afraid, the longer they leave it, that the builders are never coming back.

It's practically evening by the time I hear Ma moving around in her bedroom. The sun's starting to sink behind the buildings, and the late light coming in through the window casts a single, luminous square across the sand.

I've spent ages on the living room. I transformed the sofa into a sun lounger by spreading a bath towel over it, and I turned the thermostat up as high as it would go. For a while I didn't notice the difference, but now the radiators have started to hiss with the effort, and it's so hot in the flat I've had to change out of my clothes. I don't own a bikini, so I'm wearing my blue pyjama shorts, a training bra and a floral sun hat that I found under my bed.

For finishing touches, I've made my own seashells with cardboard and a bottle of pearlescent nail polish that I found in the bathroom. There's a sandcastle in one corner of the living room, just under the television, and I'm using Ma's mini speaker to play eight hours of Ocean Waves off YouTube on her phone.

Ma has a hard time getting the door open, because of the layer of sand. Baby? she says, as she pushes.

In here, Ma. Come look.

Ma is still only half-awake. She's wearing her dress-ing gown with the blackened sleeve that she burnt last week making pancakes for dinner. She could get a new one online, but she says she'd rather wait until the shops open.

Ma's voice comes from deep inside her throat, like the noise the kettle makes when it boils. Jesus Christ, she says. What have you done?

I stretch my arms out at my sides. I made Tenerife, I say.

Ma is quiet. She scans her eyes over the room. I think it's going to be OK, but then the corners of her mouth start to twitch. She puts her face in her hands. This means she's crying. I go to her. One of her tears falls on my shoulder and trickles down my arm.

I thought you'd like it, I say.

I can feel the sobs heaving up through Ma's chest. I press my face into her dressing gown. We were supposed to go today, I say.

Ma's breathing wobbles. I know that. You think I don't know that?

I lean back to get a look at her face. She's biting her lip, and then she screws her eyes up. I can tell she's trying to stop crying, but she can't.

I'm sorry, I say.

Ma sniffs and wipes her cheek with the back of her hand. I know, baby, she whispers.

I drop my arms down and move away from her. I look around me, at the sunken sofa with the towel thrown over, and the dull, damp sand spilt all over the floor. I had to use the mop bucket for the sandcastle, so it's turned out nothing but a shapeless heap, and my shells aren't shells at all, but pieces of litter. The Ocean Waves sound like the static that the radio used to make in the car, and the radiators have made the air wet and sticky in my lungs.

It's stupid, I say. It doesn't matter.

I kick the sand, and a chunk of it flies up and brushes against the far wall. It leaves a few grains behind, dark red against the paint.

Ma steps around me and goes further into the room. Her footsteps are muffled. I close my eyes and pinch the inside of my wrist with my nails, twisting the skin there until it stings.

Baby, Ma says, her voice softer now.

I shake my head. I don't want to talk about it.

Baby, Ma says again. Open your eyes.

Ma moves the towel from the sofa onto the floor, right into the square of light from the window. She unties her dressing gown and shoulders it off. Underneath, she's wearing her bra and knickers, tinged grey from the washing machine. She lies down on the towel, one of her arms folded back to prop up her head. Her face is slightly swollen still from crying, but she smiles, her eyes closed to the light, and her body is yellow and shining.

Come, she says. Catch the last of the sun.

ACKNOWLEDGEMENTS

There are many people without whom this book would not exist. Thank you to Steve Dearden and The Writing Squad, who do so much. Thank you to Angelique Tran Van Sang, who believed in this book when it was only scraps, and who introduced me to my exceptional agent, Niki Chang, without whom I would be lost. Thank you to Allegra Le Fanu and the whole team at Bloomsbury, for taking great care of me and my book. Thank you to all the wise and compassionate writing teachers I've had, particularly Julia Bell at Birkbeck, John McAuliffe at Manchester, and Jenn Ashworth at The Writing Squad. Thank you also to every member of those classes, who gave feedback that made me a better writer, and who shared work that I still think about. Thank you to the literary journals who published me when I was just beginning to write. Thank you to my vast and brilliant family, particularly my mother and my maternal grandmother, the two most generous people I know, for taking care of Sonny while I write. Thank you to Ella, Brenna, Masha and Lily, my best friends and the women these stories are really for, as well as my little sister Roxy, who fills me with hope. Thank you to Jacob, for being my home, and thank you to Sonny, for being the reason.

A NOTE ON THE AUTHOR

Saba Sams has been published in the *Stinging Fly*, *Granta* and *Five Dials*, among others. She was shortlisted for the White Review Short Story Prize in 2019. She is from Brighton.

A NOTE ON THE TYPE

The text of this book is set in Perpetua. This typeface is an adaptation of a style of letter that had been popularised for monumental work in stone by Eric Gill. Large scale drawings by Gill were given to Charles Malin, a Parisian punch-cutter, and his hand-cut punches were the basis for the font issued by Monotype. First used in a private translation called 'The Passion of Perpetua and Felicity', the italic was originally called Felicity.